A KILLER CHRISTMAS

NEW YORK TIMES BESTSELLING AUTHOR

CHERRY ADAIR

Have fun with Joe & Kendall
Cheers,
Cherry Adair

A Killer Christmas

This is a work of fiction. Names, characters, places and incidents are either the product of the author's imagination or are used fictitiously, and any resemblance to actual persons, living or dead, business establishments, events or locales is entirely coincidental. This edition published by arrangement with Adair Digital Press.

ISBN-13: 9781937774745

www.cherryadair.com

shop.cherryadair.com

Dedication

To my Mad Chatters who keep me sane (sane-ish!) every day.

A KILLER CHRISTMAS

SURVIVING THE HOLIDAYS CAN BE A REAL KILLER

Dispatched to an isolated ranch during a fierce Montana blizzard, T-FLAC operative Joe Zorn has been sent to protect a woman who is in impending danger. This isn't an op, but it beats spending the holidays alone at nearby T-FLAC headquarters. Things get complicated fast when the gorgeous, redhead event planner proves to be a dangerous distraction.

HOLIDAY TRIMMINGS CAN BE DEADLY SEXY

Kendall Metcalf tries to anticipate every contingency when she's commissioned to decorate a clients home for a large, weekend Christmas party. What she doesn't count on is the raging storm, or her intense attraction to the sexy counterterrorist operative who shows up unannounced. He claims he's there to protect her from the notorious serial killer obsessed with her. The killer who has escaped prison... vowing to finish what he started.

THE CLOCK IS TICKING

Stranded by the weather, anticipating the arrival of her worst nightmare, Joe and Kendall's strong attraction roars like a winter fire. Their white-hot passion is impossible to resist, but their sexual chemistry could prove a fatal distraction.

Review Snips

WHIRLPOOL Five Star GOLD. Award-winning Adair has taken readers on thrilling and wild adventures around the globe with an extremely colorful cast of characters. In the sixth and final Cutter Cay novel, she pulls out all the stops with a story that is both emotionally involving and dangerously apocalyptic! Both protagonists, Persephone Case and Finn Gallagher, are immensely engaging and their attraction is a joy to read. Adair also ratchets up the danger and intrigue as an ancient prophecy and those obsessed with it threaten them all. Kudos and thank you for a truly phenomenal ride! ~Jill M. Smith Romantic Times Book Reviews

ABSOLUTE DOUBT. Action, extreme adventure and romance. So much good stuff in this book. A counter-terrorist organization against a sociopath. A hero and heroine who both are honorable, stubborn and loyal and instantly attracted to each other. Totally loved reading this book. It is part of a series, but absolutely can be read alone. ~Fantasy Books

GIDEON. Gritty and action-packed from beginning to end, this is a classic Adair tale, so readers can be sure that the sex is sizzling and the danger relentless! ~Jill M. Smith Romantic Times 4 1/2 * top pick

HUSH Packed with plenty of unexpected plot twists and lots of sexy passion, Cherry's latest testosterone-rich, adrenaline-driven suspense novel is addictively readable. ~Chicago Tribune

HUSH delivers non-stop action, hair raising adventure, and titillating dialogue that will have readers poised on the edge of their seats waiting for what happens next. Ms. Adair has created a memorable couple whose antics are a pleasure to read about. Emotions run high in HUSH, making for an amazing read full of surprising twist and turns. ~ Fresh Fiction

Adair's BLUSH . . . sizzling chemistry adds to the heat of Bayou Cheniere, La., in Adair's knockout contemporary romantic thriller. ~Publishers Weekly starred review

UNDERTOW is full of action and suspense! Cherry Adair did such a great job making the reader feel as if they were part of the experience. I felt like I was right there diving into the water looking for the buried treasure with Zane and Teal. ~Hanging With Bells 4 Bells

WHITE HEAT "...latest in Ms. Adair's T-FLAC series, roars out of the starting gate at a fast gallop and never breaks stride in a thrilling, no-holes-barred roller coaster ride of heart-pulsing suspense and hot romance featuring a delicious, to-die-for hunk..."

"Ms. Adair skillfully weaves an exciting tale of explosive action sprinkled with twisty surprises around a sensual love story laced with gobs of fiery desire. A must for readers who like their romantic suspense hot... and the heroes even hotter!" ~Romance Reader At Heart

HOT ICE is a sure thing! Ms. Adair's characters are well supported by the secondary T-FLAC operatives that assist in the mission. The villain is equally well developed as you come to learn how a man like Jose' Morales became so twisted, that you almost feel sorry for him…almost! Ms. Adair weaves in clever tools and ingenious methods to solve this assignment. There has also been great detail given to the locations/settings, which span many continents. And the ability to bring it all together in a pulse-pounding climax will leave the reader breathless and well satisfied by the time you close this book. ~All About Romance

ICE COLD. Adair continues her wonderfully addictive series featuring the sexy men of T-FLAC with this fast paced and intricately plotted tale of danger, deception, and desire that is perfect for readers who like their romantic suspense adrenaline-rich and sizzlingly sexy. ~ Booklist

WHITE HEAT. "Your mission, should you decide to read it, is to have a few hours adrenaline pumped excitement and sizzling romance with the new T-FLAC suspense by Cherry Adair."

"You'll not want to put this book down as the plot twists come together and explode into a fantastic ending. With the spine-tingling danger, stomach churning suspense, bullets flying from every corner and red-hot romance you get White Heat. Cherry Adair has once again created a heart pounding read with extraordinary characters in extraordinary circumstances that will leave the reader hungering for more. White Heat is an excellent novel and one that I recommend as a keeper." ~ Night Owl Romance

T-FLAC Series Titles by Cherry Adair

T-FLAC/PSI

Edge of Danger Enhanced

Edge of Fear Enhanced

Edge of Darkness Enhanced

Night Fall Enhanced

Night Secrets Enhanced

Night Shadow Enhanced

T-FLAC/WRIGHT FAMILY

Kiss and Tell Enhanced

Hide and Seek Enhanced

In Too Deep Enhanced

Out of Sight Enhanced

On Thin Ice Enhanced

T-FLAC/BLACK ROSE

Hot Ice Enhanced

White Heat Enhanced

Ice Cold

CHAPTER ONE

December 20th
2135 hours
Cameron Ranch
Montana

Joe Zorn leaned into the blustery, subfreezing wind as graupel, hail-like frozen snow, slashed diagonally at his exposed skin like tiny ice darts. By any measure, nine-thirty-five on the Thursday night before Christmas, in the worst storm seen in this part of Montana in thirty years, was a massive goatfuck. The blizzard was a beast, even for a man like Joe who'd hunted terrorists in both the warmest and coldest climates on earth.

Mag light in hand, aided by the light of strings of twinkling, white 'icicles' blowing precariously from the eves, Joe did a perimeter check. Even though he'd never lived in it, he knew the house like the back of his hand. He'd built it for his wife, now *ex-wife,* Denise, a decade ago.

He found the roof of the small outbuilding housing the main generator crushed by the unusually heavy snowfall and felled by a split-in-half Ponderosa pine, brought down by the snow and high winds. *Shit.* There was an outside chance the generator might still work, but he didn't hold out much hope.

Fortunately, there were three generators dedicated to the house. The main, trashed one, out back, another that powered the security systems, and the third Denise had insisted was an absolute necessity, dedicated to her Christmas lights. Systems could be rerouted as necessary.

Stamping caked snow off his booted feet on the wide, bright red sisal doormat in front of the massive double front doors, he jiggled the iced front door handle.

As far as he knew the Camerons weren't home, and Joe didn't have a key. The wood-clad steel doors were locked, a damn good thing considering a nationwide manhunt was underway. According to his intel, a serial killer was even now finding his way, like a heat-seeking missile, through the storm to the isolated ranch, located East of Billings.

It wasn't a question of *if* Dwight Gus Treadwell aka Doctor Death, would show up to give killing event planner Kendall Metcalf another shot, it was a question of *when*.

The faint whoop-whooooop-whoooooop sound of the chopper's blades winding down followed Joe up the back steps and around to the front door. He'd landed on the snow-covered back lawn, as close as possible to the house. The chopper would've added too much weight to the snow already ten feet deep on the helipad above the garage.

A wide, covered wraparound porch circled the six-thousand-square-foot log house. Damn it, nothing like making the house a beacon for the serial killer with god-knows how many Christmas lights. It looked like the fucking Las Vegas strip squatting in the middle of remote Montana.

The wooden deck was strewn with assorted red, green and gold. Flotsam and jetsam of Christmas blew about in the fierce wind. Holding onto his fur-lined cap, Joe stepped over a still lit metal framework reindeer tethered by an electrical cord, and a sad looking Christmas tree shoved pointy end first through the spindles of the porch. The rest of the decor flew around at the whims of the raging wind. The moment he unplugged the thing, it went ass over teakettle over the railing.

While the exterior of the house was lit up, not a sliver of light escaped the tightly drawn drapes at the

windows. The glass was bulletproof. Exit *and* interior doors were wood-clad Tungsten steel, pretty much making every room in the house a "safe room," although there were a couple of those, too.

Safety precautions or not, one open window, one unlatched door, could prove fatal to the occupants of the house.

The howling wind whipped snow flurries down Joe's collar and snuck under the hem of his coat as it flapped around his ankles, making him shudder. The cold didn't bother him nearly as much as finding the place lit up like a fucking carnival.

He thumped his fist on the door again.

His assignment, the event planner, had already been here a week, decorating the house ahead of Denise and Adam Cameron's sixth annual Christmas party this weekend. She must've bought out every Christmas and craft store between Bozeman and Billings.

There was Christmas crap everywhere. Pillows had blown off the chairs that had toppled over. Area rugs- outside for God's sake- were flipped over. Scattered dirt from broken red pots that still held lit trees, decked out in twisted tinsel, made the deck gritty underfoot.

The white twinkle lights flashed on the eves, rimmed the window frames, the roofline, the doors, and every other available surface and nook and cranny, reflecting off the snow in the front yard. The lights almost blinded him.

Three hundred feet beyond the Christmas glitz, the world was pitch black. They hadn't turned on the perimeter lights. The set up was damn well perfect for anyone watching the house with a sniper rifle trained on one of the occupants inside.

Might as well have a flashing red neon arrow for Treadwell pointing to the house. *Here I am. Come and get me!*

Damn it to hell.

First up, douse the fairy lights, then turn on the powerful, motion activated halogen floods to illuminate all the way up to the treeline, fifteen hundred feet in all directions.

Joe kept one hand in his left pocket, fingers loosely clasping the grip of his custom-made HK Mark 23. Better to shoot a hole through his favorite coat than have someone open the door to find a large, armed man standing on the other side.

It worried him only marginally that he hadn't been able to contact the Camerons before he left T-FLAC

headquarters fifty miles north. High winds and snowstorms frequently messed with the cell towers way the hell and gone out here.

For all he knew Denise, Adam and the kids had returned home, and were inside, safe and warm and in the company of a serial killer's primary target. *Fuck.*

He'd tried calling the satellite phone, located in both saferooms. No response. Either they hadn't heard the sat phone ringing, or they weren't home. He'd gotten no response from Denise's mother in San Francisco either, but he'd left a message before lifting off.

Hunching into his coat, Joe jabbed at the doorbell. No corresponding ring inside indicated what he believed was the case, the main generator was down. That answered the question about its viability. "Get the lead out, people."

He had no idea how many people the woman from Fait Accompli had brought with her. Probably half a dozen assistants for him to corral and keep safe.

Not an op, but still, this was better than anticipating a frozen Christmas dinner, alone, back at headquarters.

He thumped his fist on the door a couple more times, making the oversized Christmas wreath dance. "Open the damn door!"

After a few moments he heard faint beeps from inside as the security alarm was deactivated. At least that was operational. The door swung open, spilling golden light, a rush of warmth, and the unmistakable fragrance of cookies baking onto the icy front porch. Joe's heart did a hard thump-thump as he got his first look at the Amazon in his charge.

Kendall Metcalf was luscious. Every curvy, magnificent inch of her. Her hair, the honey red of a good English orange marmalade, spilled over her shoulders like the inside of a flame. Her feet were bare, and black leggings clung like a second skin, accenting every incredible inch of her long, long, *long* legs.

A red sweater, proclaimed, in cursive white script across a mouth-watering chest; *HO HO HO Y'ALL.*

Subtly, she tucked the small gun he wasn't supposed to see in the back of her pants under her sweater, then grabbed him by the hand, practically dragging him inside.

Letting go as if remembering he was a complete stranger, she said brightly, "Yikes. You actually braved this?"

Her bone structure was elegant, the skin on her face, flawless and sprinkled lightly with tiny dots of cinnamon freckles. Scars on her hands and wrists

disappeared under the sleeves of her sweater. The scars, he knew, started at her clavicle and covered seventy-five percent of her body.

For crap sake. Get a grip, Zorn.

Those scars would remind him that she was off limits. Knowing she was marked by a madman beneath her clothes would keep his hands off her. Nothing was going to get rid of his lusty thoughts, but since he wouldn't act on them, they were his problem, not hers.

"When you didn't show up at eight I thought you'd decided not to come, and who would blame you? Did you try calling? Of course, you did. There's no service."

Her voice was naturally husky, low and unintentionally sexy. Her lips were full, and a pale, peachy pink. She seemed to smile easily as she turned to talk to him over her shoulder. Long dark lashes framed large, remarkably beautiful hazel eyes, more green than brown.

"Sorry about the atmospheric lighting, the generator conked out yesterday. Although, oddly, *some* of the lights work, and I've got all the oil lamps to see by, and the stove is gas, so I'm okay."

She'd managed to say all that in pretty much one breath. Joe took in the strategically placed oil lamps and the fire in the enormous rock-faced fireplace in the great room off to his right. There were enough pools of golden light to see by, but it left deep pockets of shadows.

She shivered hard as he paused in the still open doorway with the wind howling behind him. The garlands on the banister nearby whipped from the strong draft.

Stepping into the warmth, booted the door shut, locked it, and pressed the reactivate button on the alarm before turning around to face her. The perfumed scent of female overlaid the smell of pine, vanilla candles, and cinnamon cookies. His temperature shot up in response, heating him faster, and more efficiently, than a hot shower.

"You must be a popsicle," she said cheerfully, oblivious to his stony look. Despite the saying on the front of her sweater, her husky voice said city, not country. Her event planning business was located in Seattle.

"Let's get you defrosted." Reaching for the alarm's control panel, her hand hovered. She frowned on seeing the activation light already back on.

"Hmm." Without turning to see if he was following, she headed across the vast entry hall toward the kitchen. "Coffee."

A twelve-foot tall fir tree, covered in a mass of shiny gold ornaments was lit with tiny, flickering amber lights. It hugged the curve of the stairs beside the narrow, ten-footlong, black oak table. The surface was covered with glossy, sparkling gold and red gift-wrapped boxes, topped by an artfully arranged three-foot-high, gilded, antlered stag, and doe standing in what looked like real snow.

"I just put my millionth pot of coffee on." She didn't pause, but somehow managed to adjust one of the bows on a fake gift package in passing. "I'm always addicted when it's this cold, aren't you? I appreciate you coming out in this. As you can see, I'm up. Too much coffee, and a lot to do. Here, can I take your co - No, you're right. Keep it on until you thaw. This way."

She'd taken her sweet time answering the door, but now that he was inside, she moved at the speed of light and hadn't yet paused to take a breath. Which suited Joe just fine. He was a man of action and few words.

His hostess was still talking as she forged ahead toward the kitchen. He took advantage of her turned back to toe the riser of the third step of the wide, curved staircase. A concealed door popped open showing the hidden space. Empty. Damn.

Joe flipped it back into place with his foot. His ex-wife had a strong aversion to guns. Still, that wasn't the only place to find weapons in the house. Unless Denise had found every hidey hole and cleared them all out. A possibility with two small kids around.

"I turned every fireplace on. With these ceilings, the heat just sits there, thirty feet up where it does no good at all. The fans up there don't work without the power. The heat will eventually sink down enough that I don't have to bundle up to my frozen eyebrows while I'm w—" She stopped, turned and looked at him. "You don't care, do you?"

Since she appeared not to expect an answer, he stayed silent. The house was blessedly warm and smelled mouthwatering. The scent of Christmas was everywhere, but that wasn't the fragrance making him salivate.

She smelled as clean and fresh as. . .he frowned as he followed her into the kitchen. Some kind of. . .fruit? Yeah. Pears or something. Fresh and clean and – Jesus, he was losing it- *juicy.*

Joe found himself wanting to taste her skin to see if she tasted of pears or cinnamon and cream.

The farmhouse style kitchen, a professional chef's dream, was cluttered with a mess of used bowls,

beaters, spoons and trays of baked cookies. A basket of knitting- fluffy eye-popping pink yarn, stuck with three bright blue knitting needles, took up the seat of one barstool at the expansive granite center island. A bright yellow extreme weather coat was flung over the back of another. A dozen clear plastic tubs containing Christmas decorations were piled neatly on the kitchen table and banquette seats across the room

Organized chaos.

Taking one of the dozens of Christmas mugs off the drying rack beside the sink, she ignored the ridiculously expensive and far too complicated built-in chrome coffee making system and headed to the steaming coffee pot on the gas stove. "It took me days to learn what all those buttons were for before the power went out. It couldn't make better coffee than doing it on the stove, right?"

She carried the full mug of steaming coffee back to the center island where another half-filled mug sat beside a baking sheet of hot-from-the-oven cookies. Removing his gloves and stuffing them in a pocket, Joe puled off his hat and ran his fingers through his hair. Watching Miss Metcalf raised his body temperature several degrees above normal in no time.

She handed him the mug. "Black, I bet."

The most bizarre current of electricity passed from her fingers to his, shooting directly to his groin. At the spark, her eyes widened in surprise. She jerked her hand away. It sure as hell shocked the hell out of *him,* and he almost dropped the mug.

Joe tightened his fingers around the heat of the Christmas mug that still had a $3.99 price sticker from Ross stuck on the side. He peeled it off and stuck it on Denise's expensive, sludge green and black granite countertop. Denise did *not* shop at discount stores. Never had. The Christmas mugs must've been bought by Kendall for the weekend.

"Sorry about the sticker, I missed that one." She frowned as if leaving a price sticker on a Santa mug was a criminal offense. "That's what I thought," she said.

He hadn't opened his mouth. He presumed she was still discussing his coffee choice. "Yeah. Thanks. Where-"

"Is the family?" she finished for him.

Them, too. But he'd been referring to the cops.

"I don't actually know them. Never met them, but if this gorgeous home is any reflection, they seem like lovely people. Apparently, she and her husband took the kids over to her mother in San Francisco for the week to finish their Christmas shopping. They'll be back tomorrow morning. Although with this storm, I have to wonder if that will even be possible."

She shrugged. "I guess they'll decide tomorrow. It's been *insane* here trying to get ready for the party on Saturday, and all the houseguests, etcetera, etcetera without any help. You know how it is." She laughed, a bright, robust laugh that did ridiculous things to Joe's stomach before moving lower.

She sat her quite delectable ass half on, half off a stool, then, without looking away from his face, picked up the spatula to slide cookies from the sheet onto a plate painted with some sort of large brown, one-eyed Christmas animal. The artistic work of Joe's godson, Christopher Cameron, aged five at the time.

Her hands were pale and slender, her nails short and painted a glossy Christmas red, as were her toes. Sexy. What wasn't sexy were the defensive scars marring her smooth skin. The obscene long-ago healed wounds were thin and silvery. There were dozens of them. On the back of her hands, on her palms, on her fingers and on her wrists. Joe sucked back a black rage that surprised the crap out of him.

He didn't get emotionally involved when on an op. But this wasn't an op. Still, he was here in a professional capacity and shouldn't feel anything at all

toward the woman he was here to protect. She was a job. A non-paying, favor to a friend, one at that. Still, empathy, sympathy and a giant dose of admiration surged through him.

"Help yourself," she told him, pushing the plate an inch closer to his hand. "I just wanted a break from going up and down the ladder, and honestly? I needed a sugar hit. So cookies, because the appliances are gas."

He'd thought if the cops couldn't get to the ranch, he'd at least have Denise's husband here as back up. He and Adam had been in T-FLAC boot camp together after the Marines, and Joe trusted his friend at his back. He shouldn't have trusted his friend with his *wife*, but that was old news and water under the bridge. He didn't prod that memory like an aching tooth. He and Denise made better friends than lovers, and Adam had waited until after their divorce before making his move.

Adam had thrown in the counterterrorist towel when Denise said I do and now reveled in being a rancher. Joe valued their friendship. Hell, he was godfather to both their kids, artist Christopher, now six, and four-year-old hellion, and already a heartbreaker, Samantha.

Joe had built the house eleven years ago in the middle of prime ranch land, a great retreat for his downtime - except that he never had any downtime. Denise had ended up out here, way the hell and gone away from civilization, pretty much alone. He was a T-FLAC operative, and the giant ranch house had been constructed like Fort Knox, with enough arms and ammo inside and out to fend off a damned Mongol horde.

He'd built it with worst-case scenario in mind. An operative could never be too careful. He'd installed dozens of concealed spaces to hide weapons, and knew how to quickly access them. If the couple hadn't ferreted them out and disposed of his arsenal of weapons between his visits.

He'd sold the house and half the surrounding cattle ranch to Adam after the divorce seven years ago. They were all friends, as well as business partners. For them it worked.

"Are you alone?" he asked, straining to hear any noise to indicate someone was either upstairs or in any of the other rooms downstairs. She'd claimed she'd done all the work herself, but that could mean someone's lazy ass was elsewhere in the house. All he heard was her sudden indrawn breath over the soft singing of

Christmas carols from the emergency, battery operated, radio on the counter.

"Nope. Some of the guests arrived before the storm," Kendall said, a little more cautious now. "The guys are upstairs," she told him without a blink. She might as well have added, "Cleaning their guns."

Since *she'd* let him in instead of one of the local cops he'd spoken to en route, Joe now knew damn well she was alone. Fuck it to hell. So, they hadn't been able to make it through before the worst of the storm hit. Which meant he and Kendall were alone in the house with a killer on the loose. Clearly, she wasn't aware that Treadwell had escaped. If she was, she sure as shit wouldn't have opened the door. Still, she had that little peashooter.

He was fortunate she hadn't shot him first and asked for ID later.

If the cops couldn't get to the ranch, nobody could, not with the snow storm raging. But dollars to donuts *Treadwell* was out there. Somewhere. Storm or no storm. Joe figured they had maybe twelve hours before the situation turned to shit.

The fact that Kendall was trying to bluff him into believing she wasn't alone - now- when he was already inside and close enough to kill her, made Joe's blood

boil. Not only wasn't she supposed to be alone. She should be far, far away in an undisclosed location, under a damned alias.

Curling an arm about her waist in an unconsciously protective gesture, she held the mug to her mouth, watching him over the rim.

Joe was mesmerized by large sparkling hazel eyes staring at him unblinkingly. Her lips were a pale pink. He wondered if her nipples were the same rosy color. Jesus. He brought his erotic thoughts back in line.

She sipped coffee. "I can't *tell* you how great it is that you agreed to do this on such short notice, Don. Really. Thank you. My guy backed out at the last-"

She jumped when the oven timer let loose its alarm in a strangely karmic way as he corrected mildly, "Joe."

Her brow wrinkled briefly. "Exactly," she raised her voice over the sound of the buzzer. "Snow was *one* of Preston's reasons for not coming. But still, you'd think he'd know how to drive in a little snow, wouldn't you?"

She slid off the stool, slapped a hand on the buzzer, and grabbed a pair of oven gloves. Every vestige of saliva in Joe's mouth turned to dust as she bent over. Her heart-shaped ass, painted by black, skintight leggings, almost stopped his heart

Hellsfuckinbells. Closing the oven door, she straightened. "Still another couple of minutes. Not that we get much snow in Seattle- but still, Preston's originally from New York, so you'd think-You don't care, right?" She grinned. "Anyhoo- his rental car went into a ditch on the way in from the airport last Tuesday. Poor guy ended up breaking his wrist. And while I feel his pain, I really do, it doesn't help me with all the stuff I have to do around here.

Honestly, when you weren't here by eight, I figured the snow storm had kept you home. And since my phone wasn't working, I knew you couldn't reach me to let me know. No problem. I feel terrible that you came out in this." She gave him an earnest look. "It's dangerous out there, in this weather, especially at night."

She clearly had no idea just how bad the storm was.

"Obviously it's taken you hours to travel ten miles. I feel awful. But since you're here- The costume is on the chair over there if you want to try it on?" She indicated a red velvet suit trimmed in white fur hung over a nearby bar stool.

"Not only would I prefer not wandering around with a pillow strapped around me for the duration, but I'll be too busy bossing around the catering people on

Saturday night and won't have time to do that and be Santa, now will I?"

The buzzer beeped again, and she turned, then bent down to open the oven door giving Joe another unimpeded view of her shapely ass. He couldn't- not even in his wildest imagination, which he didn't have- envision this woman dressed in a Santa suit.

"You'd dress up as Santa?" Now a Santa suit rented from Victoria's Secret he could imagine without any problem at all.

Throwing him a look over her shoulder, she scrunched up her face adorably. "Well, yes. If you hadn't saved my bacon. I would have," she said it quite cheerfully, as she pulled out two baking sheets of golden-brown cookies. The fragrance of hot cookies, cinnamon, and sweet-scented steam filled the kitchen.

"I really appreciate that you're willing to come to my rescue like this at a moment's notice so I don't have to. Help yourself to those over near you. These will be too hot."

Hot. Definitely hot.

CHAPTER TWO

He was gorgeous in a rugged, outdoorsy, manly man way that had Kendall's pulse points racing. His shoulders looked a mile wide in his heavy, black, shearling coat, the collar flipped up around his strong, tanned throat, and fastened there with a black metal buckle. Six foot, plus, dark hair that could do with a trim. Her fingers itched to comb through the shiny strands. His shadow beard was sexy and his clear, true blue, eyes made it appear he had X-ray vision.

He was all things delicious, and she couldn't have him for a hundred reasons. Top of the list, he was married.

Kendall curled her fingers into her palm to prevent herself from reaching over to stroke him. He looked to be in his early thirties, which was surprising because his wife, Tonya, must be close to sixty. Considering the age of the sons, second husband, obviously. Hell, more power to her. *Lucky* her. He had sex appeal in spades. Kendall certainly wasn't immune.

And maybe that was why, as her body started remembering what it felt like to get pleasure not pain from a man's touch, she allowed herself a moment's fantasy. Insta-lust felt great.

Except. . .

She was delusional. Sexy and married, and in the freaking middle of nowhere. Without outside communication. This man could just as easily kill her as give her a great orgasm.

"How did you get here?" A prickle of sweat beaded around her hairline as she suddenly eyed him with suspicion, heart racing. *The past is the past. Not every man is going to hurt me.* "I don't see a snowmobile out there."

Don't get all freaking paranoid for God's sake.

Now that she thought about it - she hadn't seen or heard a blasted thing other than the wind tossing things about on the porch. The snowstorm had intensified while she was putting the first batch of cookies in the oven, the wind was wildly whipping the trees and shrubs, and the world beyond the lights of the house was dark. The house was in the middle of hundreds of acres of ranch land. No nearby neighbors to

just drop in - or to have help her when the lights had gone out.

She hadn't slept well in over a year, and she'd finally given up last night. She'd been up since five, wide awake, and filled with energy ready to tackle her piece de resistance, the giant tree in the living room. That energy had flagged hours ago, and barely half-way through decorating the tree, after multiple up and downs on the tall stepladder. After sixteen hours she was about to go up to bed, hopefully tired enough to sleep, which she'd planned to do after the last batch of cookies came out of the oven.

When she'd heard the pounding on the front door, she'd been scared half to death. Then she remembered she had no need anymore. Still. . .

She frowned. "Did Tonya drop you off?" Tonya Sanders was Don's wife. She and her sons had been here last week helping her with some of the decorating in the house after her assistant had returned to Seattle last week.

And she was babbling.

The guy - the very walking definition of the strong silent and sinful type - made her incredibly self-conscious as he watched her from steady blue eyes as she moved from oven to counter.

The ridiculously large Country French kitchen seemed to shrink with him in it. The sheer size of him suddenly made her nervous as hell. He was intimidating. She was beginning to doubt he'd fit into the rented Santa suit she'd brought with her, but she appreciated that he'd come over to at least try it on. Especially in this awful weather.

Which begged the question; why fight this seriously dangerous weather to try on a Santa suit at almost ten at night to help out a complete stranger?

None of which mattered at this point, she acknowledged. She doubted she'd *need* a Santa since according to the latest weather forecast, this storm would be with them for several days. Poor client. Denise had been so psyched for this party, but Kendall doubted any of the guests would be able to make it to the ranch now. Nor would the host and hostess.

Still, it was nice to have a bit of company after spending the past week and a half talking to herself. She wished he'd brought his wife, but she didn't blame the woman for staying in on a night like this. Was she supposed to send him back into this storm, or offer him a room here until morning? She absolutely did not want to share the house- even one of this size- with a strange man.

Even if the company in question sat still, he looked like a large wild beast in a too small cage, giving off waves of leashed energy. And Lord, he was *huge*. Kendall wasn't used to a man towering over her. But Donald Sanders did, by a good four or five inches.

Just looking at the man made her breath catch, and her heart race pleasantly. She was almost preternaturally aware of him. Of the length of his dark lashes shadowing those cool blue eyes. Of the small pale scar beside his lower lip, almost buried in the crease of his unsmiling mouth. Of the way his large, tanned hand cradled the red coffee mug.

She had a vivid, Technicolor image of that large hand cradling her breast, and felt her nipples harden and her knees go weak.

Whew! The guy was *potent*.

Kendall's physical awareness of another woman's husband filled the kitchen like a living entity, making her feel a little guilty. But, hey. What was the harm? It wasn't as though she'd *act* on the attraction she felt. It was a bit like craving a large slice of Black Forest cake when one was on a strict diet. Just because she wasn't going to eat it didn't mean she didn't want it.

Except she'd never experienced this sensation in her stomach over a piece of chocolate cake. This was

more like the dangerous excitement she'd felt as a kid, standing on tiptoe on the highest diving board. Looking down at that water miles below. Too scared to jump.

He undid the buckle at his throat. "I came by chopper."

His deep voice poured through her like hot buttered rum. He put the Christmas mug down, and shrugged out of the heavy coat, revealing an off-white wool Aran fisherman's sweater and black insulated pants. Taking off the thick coat didn't make him look any smaller, or any less intimidating. In fact, it was just the opposite. He looked even more impressive.

He was masculine in an intriguing way that had Kendall's heart doing a little hop, skip and jump. He looked as solid as a rock, with no appearance of body fat, and an impressive physique. Mouth dry, she busied herself with the cookies.

She hadn't been overwhelmed by anything other than fear in so long, this tug of attraction felt wonderful. Better because she knew there was nothing she could do about it. It just was.

"Set down in the back yard." He tossed the coat onto a bar stool beside him.

Set *what* down in the back yard?

The scent of him; clean male skin, cold night air, a hint of leather, aroused all her senses with an urgency that surprised her. Perhaps her reaction to him was due to his size. The man looked as though he could wrestle a grizzly bear. Being tall herself, it was intriguing to meet an attractive guy who was big enough to make her feel almost petite.

And they'd been in the middle of a conversation- "You came by helicopter- from next door?" Montana was huge, it made sense.

The corner of his mouth kicked up in a half smile that slid through her veins like a shot of Fireball. *Whoa. Down girl.* That small smile was potent, she wondered what it would be like full strength. Judging from her accelerated heartbeat it was probably a good thing that he'd be leaving soon. To go home to his *wife*.

"'Next door' is more than twenty miles away," he pointed out, biting into a cookie. "but I didn't— "

The house phone rang. Kendall jumped at the unexpected sound, it had been out for days. She held up a hand to stop him as she picked up the receiver. "Cameron residence." As she listened, every vestige of warmth she'd felt seconds before drained right out of her, as did most of the blood in her head.

"I know. It's been out since Tuesday. I'm sorry to hear that," she said flatly into the phone as she watched him pick up the mugs she'd bought to brighten up the dark tones of the kitchen for the weekend festivities. "No, absolutely. I quite under—" The line went dead. "stand."

Her heart was beating fast again. But this time it had nothing to do with the proximity of a sexy-looking guy. She turned away as she returned the receiver carefully to the instrument on the wall. At the same time, she lifted the back of her sweater and surreptitiously withdrew the small LadySmith handgun tucked against her skin.

Given the man's appearance, she hadn't mistaken him for a house cat. But she hadn't pegged him as a predatory tiger either. More fool her.

"*You're the best so far, ya know that?*" She could almost hear Dwight Treadwell's mild voice echoing like a never forgotten nightmare in the here and now. Obscene in this Christmas-scented kitchen a thousand miles, and a year and a half later. Goosebumps rose on her skin.

"*Defiant little bitch, ain't' ya? Your eyes say go to hell, but you're shit scared. I'm gonna enjoy this.*"

Treadwell chipped at the Formica table top with the tip of what he'd told her was his second favorite knife. There'd been nothing but mild interest in his eyes as he observed her.

There was no more room for terror in her mind. It was filled to capacity. It felt like forever since he'd grabbed her outside the grocery store and shoved her into the trunk of his car. Had no one noticed him kidnapping her? Had no one heard her screams before he'd knocked her out?

She'd woken to find herself naked, cut out of her clothes, and him standing, smiling, over her, a small scalpel in his hand. It had already been covered with her blood.

She'd screamed.

Kendall turned around to face the man in *this* kitchen. She knew her six-inch long gun only weighed about 20 ounces, but it felt as heavy as lead in her hand.

"Oh, no you don't," she snapped as he started to rise. The gun didn't waiver. "You stay right where you are. Keep your hands where I can see them."

She motioned him with the barrel. "You're not Donald Sanders. So, who the hell *are* you?"

CHAPTER THREE

Kendall thanked God she wasn't paralyzed by her fear. During her months of therapy, she'd learned that action cured fear, and inaction created terror.

Been there, done that, had the scars to prove it.

She curled her naked body protectively over her bare legs. Her skin was already slippery with her own blood where he'd repeatedly played with her with his favorite knife. Short cuts. Long cuts. Shallow. Deep. They all gave Treadwell pleasure. Each slice made her flinch and cry out. And each flinch caused the bicycle chain, used to tether her to the oven door, to rattle. She could tell that he was growing bored with the game.

He was going to kill her. Soon.

She shook herself mentally. Back to *now*. This guy didn't have to do anything to appear intimidating. He just *was*. Her stomach did flip flops, and her heart pounded as she trained the gun dead center of his chest. Big or not. A bullet would make a large hole in him. Her hand had a fine tremor she didn't care if he noticed. She didn't give a damn if he knew he scared her either. He'd know that even a bad shot from this close would kill him.

Watching him, the scar on Kendall's throat seemed to burn, and she struggled to find a balance between the knowledge that she was the one with the gun, and the memory of what a determined, violent man could do.

"Kendall," he said her name softly as he crouched in front of her, stabbing the point of his knife into the floor between her pale, curled toes so he could free his hands to reach for a large roll of canvas.

Treadwell wasn't a big man, he didn't look like a monster. He had a soft fleshy face, and flat-to-his head, light brown hair. He looked like a teacher. Or a priest. But oh God, he knew how to inflict the most exquisitely painful kind of torture. . .

The man in this kitchen was *big*. And scary looking now that she came to think about it. She realized too late that *this* was a man who could use his *body* as a weapon.

Big. Strong. Fast.

Icy sweat prickled her skin, and the residue sweetness of the last cookie she'd eaten made her swallow nausea.

She didn't have enough air in her lungs to blow out a single birthday candle right now. *Don't show fear. Don't show fear. Don't show fear.* The mental mantra worked fairly well as she tightened her grip on the gun, refusing to blink.

She'd bought the gun after the attack. She'd wanted a bigger one- a cannon. But found she couldn't handle the weight, and settled for the .22. And even though she'd gone through months of rigorous training, she'd hoped never to have to do what she was doing now. Pointing the gun at a human target.

Palpable fear made her ready and more than willing to pull the trigger, however. "Well?"

She spread her feet a little for better balance and adjusted her left hand to cup her right. "Who are you and what do you want?" She'd been expecting the neighbor's husband. He hadn't corrected her.

"Prepared to shoot to kill?" He cocked a dark brow, his tone inflexible. His deep voice reverberated through her, making the hard knock of her heart hurt her chest.

"Not just yes," Kendall said through her teeth. "But *hell* yes. I repeat: Who are you, and what are you doing here?" She still didn't bat an eyelid, and the gun didn't waver in her hands, but her accelerated, sickeningly erratic heartbeats danced behind her eyeballs.

Was he her worst fear? The realization of her nightmares?

God. She'd thought the terror was behind her. What a fool she'd been to open the door like that. Especially when she'd been here alone. But damn it, Dwight Treadwell was in jail where he belonged. He'd *never* get out. And in her own defense, law of averages wouldn't send her another attacker. Especially not all the way out here in the wilds of Montana for God's sake.

So much for the law of averages.

The question was: Run or shoot?

She debated a fraction of a second too long.

One second, he sat at the counter, the next her wrist stung as he moved across the tiled floor, brought the side of his hand down, and yanked the gun from her nerveless fingers.

He turned the barrel to point at the middle of her forehead. The small gun looked ridiculous in his big

hand. Ridiculous, but just as lethal as if he'd been holding a machine gun. He was close enough that any one of the five bullets in the chamber would kill her.

Dead was dead.

She felt the blast furnace heat of his body, he was that close. His breath smelled of coffee, his eyes were ice cold, unlike hers, his hand was dead steady. A shudder of fear rippled down her spine and settled in her churning stomach.

She had a fleeting thought. At least this would be quick.

She made a small, guttural sound as Treadwell revealed an array of sharp, shiny objects inside the unrolled canvas. She shook hard enough her teeth chattered. Tears, snot and blood mingled wetly on her face as completely mesmerized by terror, she watched him slip the first of seven instruments from their custom-made slots. He held up the thin, pointy icepick for her to see.

Blubbering like a baby, she shrank back against the dirty paneling of the trailer. "Why are you do-doing this to me?"

Treadwell's mouth twitched, the closest he came to a smile. "Because, pretty girl. I can."

If it was a choice between being shot or toyed with for hours at knife point, she'd choose to be shot.

As yet she wasn't having to make that choice. There was a third option. Run like hell. She locked her eyes with his and waited the three terrifying years it took for the first second to pass. Fear crouched in her chest, making it impossible to breathe. Soon he wouldn't have to fire the gun, she'd simply die from lack of oxygen.

"You should've shot me at the front door, Miss Metcalf. You didn't ask for ID, or anything else."

What kind of killer lectures you on safety procedures?

Through the fog of panic, she opted for another strategy. Keep him talking. She figured if he was talking, he wasn't shooting her. If he wasn't shooting her, she had a chance of escaping.

"Give me my gun back. I can rectify that mistake in a flash."

She flinched when he drew her long hair away from her neck with the cold steel barrel of her own gun. If his eyes had been chill seconds ago, when he saw the still livid scar on her throat they went Arctic. "Son of a bitch."

The scar was red and ugly. But she was alive. While he looked his fill, Kendall brought her knee up in a lightning swift move perfected in her self-defense classes.

She was quick, but he was a split second quicker. Her knee struck him in the balls, but he shifted just in time to prevent full impact. His shout of pain and his instinctive half crouch gave her just enough time to make a run for it. His hand shot out to grab her arm in passing, but she was too scared, too determined to let that happen. Again.

Having spent the last ten days decorating, and prepping for her client's Christmas house party, she knew the enormous house pretty well, He didn't.

As he gasped for air, she bolted past him. He blocked the direct route to the stairs. Kendall ran past the counter where their bright red mugs and the coffee pot still sat. Through the dining nook. Through the great room with its thirty-five-foot high limestone fireplace, soaring cedar trusses and thirty-foot tall, half-decorated Christmas tree.

Her bare feet slapped the polished wide-plank hardwood floors as she ran.*Notagainnotagainnotagain*.

With the blood rushing in her ears and her heart about jumping out of her chest like some horror movie alien creature, she heard nothing from behind her. He'd come for her, she knew, and ran faster, her brain and body flooded with acidic, pulse-pounding adrenaline.

She skirted the trio of heavy leather sofas, skidded around two tall ficus trees in their giant terracotta pots, almost careened into the ladder she'd left beside the Christmas tree, and hurdled like an Olympian over the last few, half-filled boxes of Christmas ornaments waiting to go up. While she may not be as well trained as an athlete, she was a hell of a lot more motivated.

The massive cedar staircase rose in front of her. There were eight bedrooms up there. All with solid core doors, and locks. Her breath was rapid and erratic as she started running flat out up the stairs, taking them two at a time, her heartbeat in time with the pounding of her bare feet on the hardwood.

PleaseGodpleaseGodpleaseGod-

She was half way up when his forearm suddenly hooked her around the waist. The world spun dizzily as he lifted her off her feet. At the feel of his vice-like grip around her middle, Kendall went ape-shit. Twisting and bucking, she screamed bloody murder at the top of her lungs as she tried to kick backwards.

There was, of course, no one to hear her except her attacker.

"I'm not going to hurt you," he raised his voice over her shrieks of fear and rage as he carried her,

kicking and struggling, down to the great room, and the cluster of sofas before the massive fireplace.

She'd heard that before. The words settled inside her like bricks. Stay still and suffer. She struggled and bucked as her mind raced with endless things he could do to cause her pain. Each possibility ratcheted up her anxiety causing her to fight harder as he moved toward the sofa with her flailing body hooked easily beneath one arm.

CHAPTER FOUR

Joe dropped her onto the closet sofa. She came at him with teeth and nails as he plopped down beside her in the middle of the leather sofa. "Easy. Easy- Damn it, women, no biting!" he put both hands up so she could see them.

Her fear of him broke his stone-cold heart. "I swear I'm not going to hurt you. I'm here to *protect* you, not harm you."

Too scared to listen, her pretty hazel eyes were terror-wild as she stared up at him. There wasn't a vestige of color in her face. Amber freckles stood out across her ashen cheeks like cinnamon sprinkled on fresh snow.

No good deed goes unpunished. Joe felt like a dickhead for scaring her. Feeling like a dickhead pissed him off. The fact that she could be stone fucking *dead* right now, pissed him off even more.

"You have five bullets in this peashooter of yours," he said grimly, furious at himself.

So much for his mad skills as a counterterrorist operative. He couldn't even calm down a frightened woman.

"You should've *shot* me, for Christ's sake. Don't give an attacker a chance to take the gun from you. Didn't they teach you that at- Oh, no you don't." He yanked her, as gently as possible, by her arm as she tried to make a break for it. She sank against the soft, bomber-jacket brown leather, chest heaving beneath the cheerful red sweater.

The flames in two oil lamps on the sofa table behind him flickered with his movement. More lamps around the room and gas fire bathed parts of the room in a golden glow, but left deep pockets of shadows in the corners.

"You don't think I'm going to sit here passively while you do God only knows what to me, do you?" she demanded through white lips, breath hitching. Her entire body vibrated with tension as she watched him like a mongoose watched a snake.

Joe withdrew his hand from her arm and shifted to the other end of the sofa, leaving six feet between them. She rubbed where he'd been holding her. The red

scar across her throat was good enough reason for him not to have fucking touched her in the first god damned place. He'd been away from civilized people for way too long.

He scrubbed a hand across his face. "Don't run. Please," he said quietly, dragging his gaze away from the raised, pink scar above the neckline of her sweater, made by Treadwell's scalpel. The scar was an obscenity across the smooth skin of her slender throat.

"I'm not going to sit here and chat with you before-" Her throat moved with effort then she managed thickly. "Before- *anything*."

He felt like a bull in a china shop. When the hell had this turned pear-shaped?

When he'd fucking walked in without ID-ing himself right away, that's when. "My fault. I should've told you who I was as soon as you opened the door."

"Gee. Ya think?" she interrupted, a little color returning to her cheeks. Sparks made her hazel eyes appear fiery green. "What's the plan here, pal? I'm not going softly into that good night without fighting you tooth and nail. And I *sure* as hell refuse to have a polite conversation beforehand."

"Take a breath, you're hyperventilating."

Shit. What a fucking mess. He gave her what he hoped was a benign look.

She shot *him* a look of pure loathing. Fair enough.

"You have a damned nerve waltzing in here, grabbing me like that, then trying to tell me what to do." She had to pause to take a breath. "Got to hell."

That fact that he was putting her back in hell sickened him. He pulled her little peashooter out of his belt in back. "Here."

With a heated glare, she snatched it, and flipped the safety off. Pointed the business end of it at his groin. Stripping the belt she'd used as a makeshift holster, exposed a pale sliver of her stomach. Kendall thrust the belt at him. It was warm from her body.

"Put this around your wrists."

Joe looped the belt, put his wrists through the opening, then used his teeth to snug it tightly. He didn't share with her that he'd gotten out of the pain-in-the-ass, crude but fucking effective restrains in a Columbian cartel's meth house six months ago. Getting out of this restraint was child's play.

Her shoulders relaxed some. "Talk."

"Name's Joe Zorn. ID's in my back pocket." He lifted his ass to give her access. Leaning over, she used

two fingers to slide his wallet from his pocket. Moving back to her end of the sofa, she removed his ID.

She frowned at his driver's license. "This expired three months ago."

"That's not the point. It's just ID. And for the record, I'm Denise's ex-husband. Adam and I were in the Marines and T-FLAC boot camp together. I'm a family friend."

She snorted. "*I* don't know them, so the fact that *you* do is immaterial. And frankly weird. My firm was hired by Mrs. Cameron to make this Christmas party the biggest and the best, and that's just what I'm here to do. I still don't get what *you're* doing here. Are you stalking your ex-wife?

"A mutual friend of your business partner, Rebecca Metzner, asked me to come and watch out for you. I work for a counterterrorist organization based here in Montana. T-FLAC's HQ is a helicopter ride away. I was there." In his bachelor quarters prior to the holidays, wishing to hell he had an op somewhere sunny and warm. "I volunteered. Here I am," Far from either sunny or warm. "The police will be on their way as soon as the roads are clear."

She narrowed her eyes. "I didn't hear a helicopter."

"Wind. Radio. Look out back. It's there."

"I will. But I'm not a terrorist." Folding her arms over her chest, she said flatly, "You wasted your time. What's his name?"

Following her train of thought was like watching a tennis match. He got it though. "Rick Green." The barrel of her gun still pointed unwaveringly at his balls. "He's out of the country, but he contacted me to ask - strongly- that I come here to protect you." He could practically hear the cogs of her mind sorting out who, what, where, and why.

She shot him a disbelieving look. "T-FLAC is a frying pan."

That's what she picked up on? His lips twitched, earning him a death-ray glare. "T-FLAC stands for Terrorist Force Logistical Command. I gotta tell you, getting my nads shot off isn't part of the deal, so could you point that thing someplace else?"

A .22mm at this close range didn't need the shooter to be accurate.

She lowered the small barrel, *slightly*, and scooted back into the corner of the arm of the sofa. From her uneven breathing and the tension in every line of her body, she was either poised for flight, or about to pass out from lack of oxygen. Even her marmalade hair

seemed to crackle and lift away from her shoulders, making a fiery nimbus around her head as she shifted.

Dragging in a ragged breath, she gave him a flat stare, chin tilted. Which exposed the raised red keloid tissue. "Protect me from what?"

Oh, shit. She didn't know about Treadwell's escape. Christ that scar was going to haunt him into his next lifetime. He felt too damn big. He'd been sent to guard her, and instead he'd scared the poor woman senseless.

She needed protection from her protector for God's sake.

"Who," he corrected.

Her pretty lips, just now beginning to pink up again, went white as she mouthed, "Who?"

She knew who.

She didn't notice he'd slipped his restraint as he leaned over and gently took the wavering gun from her hand, and lay it on the coffee table, before she accidentally on purpose shot him. "Treadwell."

"No!" Her hand flew instinctively to her throat. In a small voice, she said, "He's in Washington State Penitentiary."

Joe shook his head, hating to see the fighting spark go out of her eyes. "He escaped early this morning."

She wet her lower lip, clearly trying to marshal her emotions. "He's in Seattle." Pulling her bare feet up close to her body, she hugged her knees with her arms and gave him a look that sent shards of ice through Joe's veins. A look that said she knew she wasn't safe. Anywhere. "He wouldn't think to look for me in Montana."

She crossed one pale, slender foot over the other, curling her toes defensively. Joe frowned at how ridiculously. . . *vulnerable* her feet looked. He dragged his gaze back to her face.

Her large, now more-green-than-hazel eyes glittered. Not with tears, but with fury. "That psycho knows where I am, doesn't he?"

Without a doubt. Joe practically heard shark music as the son of a bitch got closer. "The guards tossed his room after he escaped early this morning." He kept his voice calm and even. "They found a copy of the Seattle Post Intelligencer. One article had been torn out."

She blanched. "THE ONE WHO GOT AWAY. Local Event Planner Returns To Work fifteen months after harrowing ordeal with serial killer Doctor Death."

She quoted as if reading the headline. "The paper published that last week in their society pages."

He nodded. "Yeah. The article was pretty detailed. He knows about Denise's party. And the location." Sheer, unadulterated terror showed in her expressive eyes.

Shit. Shit and double shit.

"H-he promised at his sentencing that he'd find a way to kill me." Kendall hugged her calves even tighter. From her tone and the haunted look in her eyes, Joe figured she'd replayed that ugly moment in her mind a million times.

Just seeing the photographs from Treadwell's crime scenes were enough to turn Joe's stomach. She was lucky, *damn* lucky to be alive.

He was here to make sure she stayed that way.

"I built the house before Denise and I got married," he told her, trying not to inhale the heady fragrance of pear intensified by her fear. Of him.

He had no damned right to be this turned on by a woman he'd just scared to death. Not to mention a woman afraid for her life.

He kept his voice even and low. His job here was to keep her safe, and unafraid, not want to jump her bones, or scare her half to death. Fuck. Talk about inappropriate. "Working for T-FLAC, I knew she'd be alone a lot."

She frowned at the non sequitur. "Is that why you got divorced?"

"One of many reasons. I'm gone a lot. The point I'm trying to make is, being in the business I'm in, this house is fortified. Steel encased doors, bulletproof windows, weapons galore and vantage points. One of two safe rooms is through the pantry next to the kitchen. It should still be filled with weapons."

"And?"

"I'm just here as a precaution. Think about it. Treadwell is on the run with no money, no nothing. He'll be recaptured soon but until then, I'm here to stand between you and that fucker if he *does* show up."

#

"I appreciate the sentiment, but seventy-two-hours, a *lifetime* in Kendall Marie Metcalf years, being taunted by that lunatic before he slashed my throat taught me there's no such thing as *safe*."

Her mind shied away from the memory of that hellish eternity spent with Treadwell. Without conscious thought, she lay her hand protectively against the base of her throat as she scanned the great room with a professional eye. Suddenly, coming back to work only

fifteen months after her kidnapping and attack, seemed way too soon.

Not enough therapy. Not enough physical healing. Not enough time.

She wasn't freaking *ready* to face Treadwell again. Not. Ever.

Mentally she started making a list of what had to be done before she could leave. A coping mechanism she'd perfected in the last few months. She'd discovered that if she kept her body and mind busy enough, she could keep the horrific memories at bay. *Almost.*

That's what she had to focus on now so she didn't lapse into a full-blown panic attack.

She'd been so tired. So terrifyingly debilitated by her terror for those hours with Treadwell, that she'd almost pleaded with him to end it.

"Beg me."

"Go to hell."

He positioned the scalpel over her left breast and applied just enough pressure for the tip to pierce her skin.

Her own shrieks echoed and re-echoed in her head, but she was incapable of sound now.

He did it again and again, decorating her torso with a neat pattern of dots. Each dot burned like fire.

"Beg me now, pretty girl," he whispered, leaning close to her ear. His moist, fetid breath brushed her cheek.

"F-fuck you." *Stop. Stop. Stop!*

"He won't get through *me,*" Joe's eyes were a hard, flat blue, his tone resolute. "And the local authorities are aware and will be here as soon as they can get through."

Her mind skittered from fear to who *is* this guy? And then to something she was in control of. The tree.

The almost decorated thirty-foot Douglas fir she'd been working on just before her coffee break almost touched the soaring wood-timbered vaulted ceiling and still had to be finished. Three hours. Tops. The bedrooms were ready for the onslaught of guests, the mantles- oh blast it- except for the one in the small downstairs office, were done. That one would take at least an hour.

Good God! What the *hell* was she thinking? She jumped to her feet. Ready for action when there was no action to be taken. "We have to tell the Camerons to cancel the party."

Kendall didn't *want* the party cancelled. This was one of Fait Accompli's biggest events, and a feather in their cap. She and her partner Becky had been thrilled

with the article in the local paper. Great P.R. and the chance to attract more high-end clients.

The awesome article had attracted the attention of Treadwell.

"With this storm I'm sure they've already done so," he told her. "Nothing's moving out there. No signal." He held up his phone, looking no more pleased than she felt.

"The helicopter," she asked desperately, heart pounding so hard she felt each throb jarring her very bones. Even though she stood still, Kendall's insides ran, trying to escape.

He shook his head. "*I* barely made it here. The rotors started freezing over ten miles out. The snow's already ten feet deep and getting deeper. I've never experienced a winter as bad as this, and I've lived in Montana most of my life. Took me a good ten minutes to walk from the back to the front of the house," he told her.

"It's gotten considerably worse since then. Blizzard conditions, and dangerously high wind advisories. They're instructing everyone to stay indoors for at least the next eight to twelve hours. And even then, the roads are impassable and will need to be

plowed before anyone can travel any distance. Right now, the weather is our friend."

Kendall used a finger to separate a space in the white linen drapes so she could see outside. The snow-covered trees and shrubs in the front yard were mere clumps of white, illuminated by the dancing Christmas lights she'd had four handymen string all over the exterior of the house last week. So much for that. As the high winds continued, they were already being ripped from the eves. The slanted and thickly falling snow was a white veil drawn across a black world.

Was Treadwell even now watching her? Her mouth went dry, her body cold. She snugged the drapes closed, then walked back to sit on the arm of an adjacent sofa, a good twenty feet away from Joe.

"We could go to one of the outlying guest cottages," she suggested hopefully. "He wouldn't look for me there."

"First, you couldn't be any safer than you are here, in this house, with me. And we wouldn't make fifty yards out there in this weather."

Kendall jumped to her feet again and started to pace out the excess energy caused by the fear jangling her nerves. It was a nice big room, and she lengthened her stride, mind racing as she took a turn around the

stepladder and walked around stacks of plastic containers filled with Christmas decorations.

"Thank God the storm prevented any of the houseguests from arriving early."

Had she taken all the flower arrangements from the mud-room to the bedrooms? She'd better check.

Who the hell *cared*? No one was coming. She didn't have to complete the tree or put fresh flowers in the guest rooms. She didn't have to do anything because not even the host and hostess would be here on Saturday.

Joe rose, withdrawing a large, nasty looking black gun from the waistband at the small of his back. It looked mean, and powerful, and as if it meant business. Very much like the man carrying it.

Even with Joe and his big gun here with her, her body was taut with fear. Memories of Treadwell and what he'd done to her were as much a part of her now as her distinctive red hair.

She counted her own heartbeats as Joe stood in front of her.

"Come with me." Picking up her small gun from the coffee table, he handed it to her. He waited while she tucked it into the elastic waist of her leggings, then started walking, clearly expecting her to follow.

He picked up one of the half-dozen oil lamps she'd set out while she was going up and down the stepladder. "We'll check all the windows and doors, and I'll show you where more weapons can be found. Denise got rid of most of them because of the kids, but there are still plenty around. "

"I'm right behind you." She wasn't much of a follower, but where Joe and that cannon went, so goeth Kendall Metcalf. They went to the kitchen first. The smell of cookies was so normal, so everyday, the radio was softly playing; *Grandma got run over by reindeer.*

Kendall turned it off to save the batteries. "I already did all that," she told Joe as he fiddled with the latches on the bay window overlooking the snow blanketed front yard.

"And I'm double checking."

"Fair enough."

Dwight exchanged the small paring for a bigger knife, pausing only long enough to wipe the flecks of dried blood from his previous toy on her bare leg. She screamed in earnest when he started taking shallow slashes at her skin as he connected dots in an obscene, scarlet geometric pattern.

She'd blacked out.

Filled with dread and foreboding, Kendall froze beside the center island. "Oh, God," it was almost

impossible to push the words from her frozen lips. "He's here."

"Not possible," Joe assured her. "Go and turn-

"The outside lights off." She was already striding toward the pantry where that control panel was located. She turned to look at Joe. He'd stopped dead in the middle of the kitchen. "Coming?"

"Yeah." His eyes looked a little glazed, his voice sounded hoarse.

Kendall shot him a worried glance. "You're not sick, are you?"

He swiped a large hand across his jaw. "I'm fine. Hit those lights, I want to get cracking and check upstairs."

He sounded as if he were coming down with a cold. Which was unfortunate. Because just looking at him made *her* feel hot all over despite her fear. Clearly she'd lost her ever-loving freaking mind.

She'd felt zero sexual desire in over a year. Not a flicker. Not even a nanosecond of thought. Yet here was this giant of a man, with his dangerous eyes, and his sexy mouth and all she could think of was wanting to climb his body and kiss him.

Treadwell was on his way. Nothing would stop him. If he wasn't nearby now, he would be *soon*. All that stood between her and a serial killer, was Joe.

She shook her head. She was really losing it if she was this tempted to jump the bones of a man she'd just met. She hadn't had any intimate relationships since. . .*Then*. But prior to her kidnapping, she'd had two fairly long-term relationships in the prior ten years. But she'd dated Greg for a year, and Mark for more than six months, before sleeping with either of them.

She just wasn't that spontaneous. She liked to think things through. Weigh the pros and cons. Deliberate her options. Kendall bit her lip as she pondered this weird anomaly brought on by Joe Zorn.

Part of it, she admitted was the latent strength and power exuding from him like heat from the sun. It wasn't just that now he'd explained who and what he was, she did feel safe. He'd pushed her previously invincible self from out of the shadows into startling daylight.

That in itself was a big turn on to a woman who'd begun to believe her fear was part and parcel of who she'd become. A big turn on that grabbed her sexual desire and shook it the hell awake. But she didn't

trust easily, and doing so now was a monumental risk. One that she had to take.

The scars Dwight Treadwell had inflicted on her weren't all on the outside.

"The Christmas lights are on a different, dedicated generator." Joe followed her to the door of the walk-in-pantry and waited in the doorway while she dealt with all the plugs and switches for the outside Christmas lights.

He didn't offer to help her, and she was grateful. She needed to keep busy.

"Move over to the shelves." He entered the small room, and she backed up. He seemed to suck up all the oxygen.

"This is one of two panic rooms," he told her, seemingly unaware that she was having difficulty breathing. "The other's on the second floor through the master bedroom closet."

Better to look around than at him. Kendall bet he wasn't aware of how that slight wave in his dark hair softened his features and made him look like not such a hard ass.

Better not think about his ass.

The pantry didn't look like a safe room. But then she had no idea what a safe room was supposed to look

like. But certainly not as though the owner had just done an annual Costco run stocking up on basics. Ceiling to floor shelves on two sides, an electrical panel that had seemed insanely large when Kendall had first seen it, and a giant French door freezer which shared a wall with the door.

The room shrank dramatically in size when Joe shut the door behind him. He stayed near the door, gaze steady. "Reach under the right-hand side of that shelf with the paper towels. Feel a button?"

Kendall nodded when she touched a cool, smooth, round button about three inches across.

"Press it."

She did so. A four-foot-wide by eight-foot high section of the shelves slid backward, then soundlessly to the side, and out of sight.

"Wow." The exposed room was shallow- maybe three feet deep, but the top portion was filled with an astonishing array of guns, rifles, and assorted things Kendall couldn't identify, neatly hung on hooks on the pegboard. The bottom half held an impressive selection of wines.

"Good," Joe crossed the pantry, not commenting when Kendall moved well out of his way. "Almost as I left things. "

"Wine and weapons. Healthy combo," she said, her tone dry. "You expected a war?"

"I always expect a war and am rarely disappointed. Plenty of MRE's in that box on the floor, as well as basic first aid supplies, should the need arise. Both safe rooms are indestructible. The wine cellar component was Denise's AD addition."

"AD?"

"After divorce."

"I'm surprised they left any of these guns here with kids in the house."

"They don't need all the safety features I left behind. I get it. They don't have terrorists hunting them."

"But you do?" Kendall shook her head when he shrugged. "You live a terrifying life."

"As I said, I always look at the worst-case scenarios. That way, I'm never caught unaware. You only have five rounds. I presume you know how to use it and load it?"

She always considered worst case scenarios, too, in that regard they were very similar. God, she was so freaking *sick* of living this way. "I do."

"Do you want to exchange it for something with more firepower?"

Looking at the neatly stored weapons was mind-boggling. There must be thirty guns concealed behind the canned and paper goods.

"Tempting, but I'm intimately familiar with my LadySmith. I've practiced for hours almost every day for over a year, and I'm a damned good shot. Tempting as all of these are, this isn't the time to try something new and unfamiliar. Unless you have something like a surface to air missile in here with Treadwell's name on it?"

"On the roof."

Kendall blinked. "Seriously?"

"It doesn't have his name on it, but it'll do the job if need be."

"Comforting thought."

He removed a box of ammo from one of the metal racks, then tipped half a dozen .22's into his palm before handing her the box. "Bring this with us," he instructed, then placed the handful of bullets on the shelf holding canned fruit just inside the door. "Right here should you need them."

If her heart beat any harder or faster she'd have lift off. Kendall pushed words out of her dry mouth. "So, despite all the high-tech safety precautions, you believe someone can *still* gain entry?"

Someone. Treadwell.

"I'm a glass half empty guy. Rather be over prepared than not."

Now she knew that Treadwell was on his way, and despite all of Joe's James Bond precautions, there was a possibility, no matter how damned small- that the serial killer could get into the house.

Got it.

"The pantry door, like all the other doors in the house, is encased in impenetrable tungsten steel," Joe told her, seemingly oblivious to her distress. "Can't be kicked in, or shot through. All lock from both inside and outside the same way. See right here?" He showed her an ingenious locking device cleverly hidden inside the door frame. If one didn't know it was there, it was unlikely anyone would notice it.

"Shut the door, then pull up and out like this." He closed the door, then showed her how to activate the locking device. "Unlocks like this." He unlocked, then reopened the door. "Show me."

Kendall did so. He made her do it twice more.

"Do all these clever safety precautions work if the Christmas generator goes out?"

"The security systems work off a separate generator. They won't go down even if everything else does."

"There are *three* generators in the house?"

"Yeah. In the unlikely event Treadwell gets into the house," he told her as she unlocked the door, then pushed it open. "First course of action, if possible, is run like hell. If you can't get *out*, lock yourself in any room, and wait for help."

Instinctually her hand went to her throat, and she asked, voice thick with dread, "Where will *you* be?"

"In the highly unlikely event we become separated."

Which really, really didn't answer the question.

No. No. No.

"So, you not only expect him to break into this Fort Knox, impenetrable house filled with bullet proof freaking doors and arsenals of weapons everywhere, you think he's going to kill *you*? Dear God. . ."

He shook his head. "*Worst case* scenario."

Treadwell will break in. Joe will die. I'll die.

Kendall began to hyperventilate. Lightheaded she pressed her fist against her racing heart.

"Hey hey hey." Suddenly he was right there, taking her into the circle of his arms. His hold was light,

barely there, but Kendall shoved her palm against Joe's chest, unable to bear a physical touch.

"Honey, I swear to God." His hold lessened, but his arms still caged her body. "No one can get into the house, nor will he get within a mile of you. If you keep doing this, you'll pass out."

She barely made sense of his words, her brain filled with visions of pain, blood, and bone-chilling fear. She felt the up and down motion of his palm on her back as if through an insulated jacket as her breath grew more and more rapid. Black spots danced like a snow flurry in her vision.

Dropping his arms, he reached down to take her limp hand then placed it palm down on his chest where his heart beat steadily. "Shit. You hold onto me then," he took her other hand and placed that on his chest, too. "Breathe, sweetheart. Breathe. I'm right here. No one will hurt you. No one."

Joe kept talking, but Kendall's lizard brain couldn't compute the words.

"Shh shhh shhh," he murmured against her numb mouth, sipping her uneven breaths as he pressed his lips to hers.

It was kiss her, or watch her hyperventilate until she passed out.

At first there was zero response as her soft, cool lips trembled with her struggle to draw in enough oxygen and her glazed eyes looked right through him.

Joe slid his palm under the warm silk of her hair to stroke her nape, deepening the pressure of his mouth until he felt a slight hitch in her erratic breathing. Years of experience as a counterterrorist operative made him hyperalert to her smallest sign that holding her brought on more distress.

He deepened the kiss by the tiniest degrees, listening to the rate of her breathing, gauging the temperature of her slowly warming skin, feeling the rapid beat of her heart, like a tiny, terrified bird, fluttering against his chest.

Joe swept his tongue into her mouth. She stiffened, then gradually relaxed against him, her tongue sliding against his. With each glide of tongues, she relaxed against him more and more. Joe waited until her arms went around his waist before he tightened his arms, leaning back against the wall, cradling her in the V of his legs.

This time her breath was coming faster from desire, and he knew she'd managed to conquer her panic

attack. With a slow brush of his closed mouth across hers, he lifted his head. A little pink was coming back to her white cheeks.

Slowly she lifted her long lashes to look up at him.

Holding her gaze- noting that her pupils were now reactive, he stroked strands of copper hair off her still clammy cheek with his finger. "Better?"

She nodded, but didn't move out of his hold. "Sorry. I haven't had one of those in a while."

Joe wanted to taste more of the cinnamon on her lips, but he kept his hold light and impersonal and didn't dive back in for a more passionate kiss. "Understandable under the circumstances."

The second he felt her body shift, he dropped his hands and let her step away.

"I never tried a kiss to deal with my panic attacks." Her pure smile did something weird to Joe's heart. "It was very effective. Thanks."

He didn't ask how frequently she had them, or what the fuck she did when she had them when she was alone. "Any time." He straightened from his slouch against the wall.

"Let's finish up here, then I'll take you through the rest of the house. The Camerons removed most of

my shit after the kids got here, more now the little buggers are ambulatory. But Adam was in the military, and way out here he knows to be well armed. He wouldn't've stripped out everything. Let's go find out what we have to work with and talk strategy. You good?"

The color had returned to her fair skin, and her hazel eyes looked bright and focused. "Yeah. Freaking out isn't my usual way of dealing with stress. What next?"

"The monitors show every side of the house from various angles." He switched each screen on, Click. Click. Click. There were eight screens about the size of large iPads. The pictures were normally crystal clear, but now all he saw was the white-out.

He transferred the feed to his smarter-than-most phone so he could monitor the perimeter from wherever he was in the house. Although the silent alarms would let him know when the motion sensors where tripped.

"Satellite phone here hooks directly into the control center at T-FLAC." Joe plucked it off the holder on the wall. It was immediately answered by his Control, Doug Silva. "Silva."

Joe put the sat phone on speaker. "Update on our target?"

"In the wind."

"Fuck, Silva. We should have the bastard in hand by now."

"No shit. Last sighting, he was holed up in a motel five miles east of Boise, Idaho," Silva sounded as cool and as impersonal as he always did, but a sliver of frustration colored his voice. "No vehicles reported stolen, doesn't mean he hasn't found transportation of some kind, but at this time, with more of the storm bearing down, there are no vehicles on the roads. Temp is minus thirty degrees, windchill—lethal, plus twelve inches of fresh snow. Place has come to a literal standstill. No one in or out. Prediction; roads expected to be cleared within twenty-four hours. Your guy isn't going anywhere until then.

Joe didn't ask what shit a bored serial killer could do when caged like a rat and his bait was six hundred, inaccessible, miles away.

Joe finished the call. "They'll catch him."

"It might be impossible for anyone else to leave Boise, but don't doubt for a moment, that he'll *find* a way," she told him. "He stalked me for *three weeks* before he took me, in broad daylight, outside the grocery store, on a busy Saturday morning, with a parking lot full of cars and people."

She hugged herself, unconsciously self-soothing by rubbing her upper arms. "He's incredibly, *terrifyingly*, focused and detail driven. He was a Physician Assistant in the same medical offices as my doctor. He saw me coming out of the building and followed me home that day, biding his time. By then he'd already killed a dozen other women."

By the time he'd taken Kendall outside the grocery store, Treadwell had already killed twenty-three redheaded women. The authorities had proof, they just hadn't found the bodies. Yet. Still, he'd been convicted on the bodies that *had* been discovered.

"He knew where I lived." Her anguished voice broke Joe's heart. "He k-knew where I worked. The names of my, my friends and coworkers. All the doctors in that building were networked. He had access to all my personal information."

She shuddered. Because of his medical training, he knew exactly where to slice to inflict the most pain just short of death." Her throat worked and she rested her hand over the scar.

Joe had been briefed. Treadwell's psychoses had been exacerbated by his drug addict, redhead mother who'd violently abused him until he killed her when he

was fifteen. It had taken him nine fucking days to carve her up. He'd enjoyed every moment.

"He knows where I am, Joe. He *will* come."

Yeah, he would. T-FLAC had Treadwell under tight surveillance. The second the man made a move, Joe would be alerted. "And when he does, we'll be ready for him."

#

Once Joe showed her everything the safe room had to offer, Kendall held onto the satellite phone as they returned to the kitchen. One more thing tucked into the elastic waistband of her leggings and she'd be walking around with a bare bottom.

She was so filled with nervous energy, she didn't know what to do with herself. She licked the taste of him off her lips as she crossed to the counter and started cleaning up the mess she'd made earlier when she'd started stress baking.

"What are you doing?"

Trying not to freak out. Reliving that incredible kiss. Finding something to do with my hands instead of holding on to you. Pick one.

Placing the cooled cookies in an airtight container, she glanced at Joe over her shoulder.

"Cleaning up my mess before I go up and change. I have nowhere to tuck my gun and the phone."

His gaze drifted to her mouth, and something elemental sparked between them. He hadn't moved from the doorway, but Kendall felt crowded, breathlessly so. He lifted his eyes back to hers. He wasn't getting out of the way, and she started to move past him. "I have a billion things to do."

"No, you don't."

Stopping mid-stride, her shoulders slumped. "Right. Still, the Cameron's paid Fait Accompli. The least I can do is clean up and take everything down before I leave. It would be terrible for them to come home after Christmas to find all the decorations are still up after the holidays are over."

"There's plenty of time to do that."

She forgot what she'd been about to say, her breath stopping altogether at the blaze of predatory heat she saw in his eyes. The smell of him; damp wool, clean skin, *male,* was intoxicating and made her giddy with longing.

She ached to slide her hands under his sweater so she could touch hot, bare skin. She wanted to stand on her toes and press her mouth to his. God. She wanted him to kiss her again until she forgot why he was here.

Amusement danced in the smoldering flame of his blue eyes, but he didn't smile back. "We've known each other all of- what? An hour? And I already know a lot about you."

Only an hour? The blizzard had caused her to lose track of time, but it *was* almost eleven. Joe had only arrived barely an hour and a half ago.

"Oh, yeah?" She dragged in a ragged breath. "Like what?" It was almost impossible to have a coherent thought when all her senses were on overload. The smell of him, the strength of his hand on her arm, the radiant heat of his big body so close to hers- all conspired to make Kendall's brain fog up.

"You babble when you're nervous."

Since right now she was pretty much speechless with lust, she blinked. "*Excuse me*? I don't *babble*. . .Okay, yes, guess I do. Sometimes."

"You make busywork when you're scared."

That too. She narrowed her eyes and glared at Mr.-Know-It-All. "So? I also own my own, very successful business, make *the* best homemade chili, and knit sweaters people would pay big bucks for. What's your point?"

His gaze moved over her face in a disconcertingly thorough sweep as though he were

memorizing each feature, every freckle. Kendall's breath caught in her throat as their bodies seemed to gravitate closer without them actually moving their feet.

"I bet your bras match your panties."

Now *that* came out of left field. It also jumpstarted her heart as though she'd been resuscitated. Holy cow. "That's an incredibly personal observation for a stranger to make," she told him primly. "And by the way. You'd be wrong. I don't wear panties." A thong, but not panties.

"Ah, Jesus." He choked back a laugh. "No fair." Still smiling, his big hands framed her face, then he touched a gentle hand to her hair. "I've never seen hair this unusual color. An intriguing mixt of all the colors of Fall. Now my favorite season." His voice was husky, thick with desire.

A desire Kendall, too, felt.

He stroked his hand down the glossy curtain, then curled his fingers beneath the strands to cup the back of her head, drawing her toward him.

"You have the most beautiful hair." He brought a handful to his face, rubbing the bright strands against his skin. "Silky. Smells like pears. Delicious." He sifted the filaments through his fingers, watching intently as

they drifted to cling to her shoulders and front of her sweater.

He traced her lower lip with his thumb, then bent his head and kissed her as if he were a starving man at a feast. The pleasure of his open mouth on hers was so intense Kendall went deaf and blind with it. His lips were firm, his taste heady, and the unexpected intimacy of his tongue curling against hers was shockingly sweet.

Oh, Lord, that feels so good. Wonderful. Amazing.

Fisting his hands in her hair, Joe pushed her back against the doorframe, kissing her with the same urgency she felt. He pressed his knee to the juncture between her thighs. She whimpered with relief, clutching at his arms for balance as he drew her against the muscled plane of his chest.

She needn't have bothered. Joe wrapped his arms around her and held her tightly against him until their heartbeats echoed one another.

She went up on her tiptoes, wrapping her arms around his neck, eagerly pressing her mouth to his. Eyes closed, her senses flooded with the taste of him as he explored her mouth. There was nothing tentative about the kiss. Apparently he'd been left as unsatisfied from the pantry kiss as she.

She made a soft, inarticulate sound of need, of hunger, her soft breasts pinned against the hard plane of his chest.

For three minutes Kendall forgot she was the prey of a determined serial killer

CHAPTER FIVE

"I wish to hell I *could* get you out of here now," Joe told her as they went upstairs. She accompanied him from room to room while he checked locks on all the windows and doors. She didn't need the added knowledge that Treadwell was on a killing spree en route because of her.

Treadwell's preference was redheads, like his mother. But this time around he'd widened his choice to anyone who got in his way due to his time constraints and the ferocity of the weather impeding his travel.

Joe considered the fact that *he'd* made it here against the odds. He had to trust that his people would track Treadwell down. Again. But given the weather conditions, satellite surveillance was iffy, and they had no one boots on the ground following him.

He didn't *feel* anyone out there. Not yet. Considering the ferocity of the storm, coupled with numerous roadblocks it was perhaps too soon. But Joe could easily imagine the sleaze hiding out in the dark, biding his time, waiting for just the right moment.

The house was as secure as Fort Knox. He'd built it with attack in mind, knowing Denise would be here alone when he was on an op. Should a tango discover where he lived, his wife could hold them off until help arrived.

As a cattleman, ex-marine and ex-T-FLAC operative, his friend Adam knew the value of high security. He'd left most of Joe's toys where Joe had left them. Just removing anything the kids might come across.

He and Kendall listened to the weather forecast on the emergency radio, this part of the state had come to a complete standstill for the next twelve to twenty-four hours.

When the call from fellow operative Rick had come earlier that day, Joe had just returned from an op in Thailand. He'd taken only enough time to grab appropriate cold weather gear, and haul ass to the airfield where he'd commandeered a chopper, to attempt beating the storm.

On arrival at T-FLAC airport, he'd been cautioned about flying in this weather, flown anyway, just making it in the zero visibility. The massive

snowstorm had swept in more quickly than predicted. The full fury had hit just as he landed, and from the sound of it howling outside the windows, was rapidly worsening, and pelting the glass with sleet, was rapidly worsening.

"I'm willing to take the risk of leaving now," Kendall told him as she rubbed her arms as if she were cold. The house was a comfortable seventy degrees with all the fireplaces on. "Of course, I wouldn't want you to do anything dangerous."

Joe smiled, touching a finger to her pale cheek. "Sweetheart, I *live* for danger. If I thought we had a snowball's chance in hell of making it out of here, we'd be long gone. But it would be suicide trying to fly in this, the snow's too heavy, the wind's too high."

He'd been damn fortunate he'd been able to land in the high winds and blinding snow swirls earlier. The storm was considerably worse now. He'd known that there would be no way to get her out until the storm let up some. Known it, but sure as hell hadn't liked it.

"There are snowmobiles in the garage."

He knew. "Like I said, if I thought we had a shot, believe me, we'd take it." They weren't going anywhere just yet, but somehow, he'd get her out before Treadwell found his way to the Cameron's ranch.

"As long as *we're* gone before he shows up," Kendall muttered, reading his mind. Again. "If we can't leave because of this snowstorm, he can't get here. Right?"

For all he knew, the son of a bitch was already halfway to the ranch. Treadwell was highly motivated. Kendall had identified him unequivocally and put him in prison.

She was his only failure.

His unfinished business.

"One would hope." Joe twisted both locks on an upstairs bathroom window. Everything was firmly locked, but he checked and double checked anyway. The room was small, especially with both of them in it. He was becoming addicted to the fresh, crisp fragrance of pears. The kisses downstairs seemed to have happened years ago instead of less than ten minutes. He wanted more than to taste her mouth.

He wanted to feel her bare skin against his. He wanted to taste her all over. He wanted to feel the weight of her breasts, and taste her nipples against his tongue.

It's good to want things, he thought wryly.

Kendall straightened up a basket of luxurious toiletries on the counter. "I hope they got hold of the

guests to tell them not to come." She refolded two perfectly folded towels, smoothed them flat, then hung them back over the rod.

"Don't worry about it. Denise will have done that when she saw the weather reports."

"Of course." She was so filled with nervous energy he wondered if he should suggest they go down to the gym in the basement. She could run a few hundred miles on the treadmill. That might tire her out-although Joe had some better ideas on how he could channel some of that frenetic energy.

Biting back a smile as she refolded a point in the edge of the toilet paper, he motioned her out of the small bathroom. She scanned the guest room before exiting, turning left down the wide hallway. A single strand of her long hair clung to his sweater as she passed, and stuck there, tying them together, as he followed her down the hallway lined with family pictures.

Next to the blissfully happy photograph of Denise and Adam's no-expense-spared wedding, was one of himself and Denise at *their* hurry-the-justice-of-the-peace-is-waiting wedding.

The fact that they were all good friends hadn't changed with either marriage.

Holding up the lamp, Kendall stepped closer to look at the photographs. Her hair caught the light and shone in shades of glossy ginger, gold, a deep amber. She had beautiful hair, very touchable. Joe stuffed his fingers in his front pockets.

Slowly walking down the corridor, she paused now and then, to take a closer look. “Denise is very attractive.”

Denise was a stunning, petite blond. “She’s lovely inside and out, and doesn’t give a damn that people stop in the street to stare at her,” Joe told her, wishing Kendall wasn’t so damned appealing herself. "Her looks meant nothing to her, and half the time she wears her hair in a haphazard ponytail, no makeup, and dresses in ratty jeans and T-shirt.”

Joe had dated women both beautiful and plain over the years. He’d been attracted to them for things other than their looks. Kendall was in a whole other league.

“We've been friends in first grade, and it seemed inevitable we get married. But as Denise said when we divorced, we didn’t have the fire necessary to take us from friends to an old married couple. I’m glad she found that person in Adam.”

This attraction for Kendall couldn't come at a worse time and/or place. "She was a cosmetics model for a while and hated it. She's taken to being a rancher's wife very well, and she's an amazing mother. She always wanted kids. Sam here, is her spitting image."

He indicated the photograph of Samantha atop the sorrel quarter pony he'd given her. "Her fourth birthday present."

"That looks more like a grimace than a smile. Poor baby was scared on that big horse."

With a smile, Joe shook his head. "She was pissed because Adam wouldn't let her gallop her new horse across the fields. *Alone.*"

Kendall gave him an amused glance. "You adore her."

"Crazy about both kids. I'm their godfather, actually."

"Do you see them often?"

"Whenever I'm in town." Joe enjoyed the opportunity to watch Kendall unobserved as she examined the framed photographs. "Adam and I are partners in the ranch. Angus beef cattle. Good investment for when I can no longer haul ass in places where the bad guys outnumber the good guys. T-FLAC headquarters is only fifty miles away."

Her hair slid over her arm as she tilted her head, looking at the top row of pictures. “She keeps a photograph of her first wedding up on the wall with those of her *second* wedding? That’s very progressive of her.”

“We make better friends than spouses. Adam has loved Denise since fourth grade. The Cameron’s are family.”

They got to the other end of the wall of family photographs in the upstairs hallway. “No other family?”

“Only child. My folks died six months apart, ten years ago. Mom of a massive heart attack, my dad in a boating accident.” Joe had never been sure that it *was* an accident, but the end result had been the same.

“That’s awful. I’m sorry.”

“Yeah. Thanks. So was I. I don’t think they could’ve made it without each other. What about you? Family?”

She hesitated for a moment as they passed the closed doors of several guest suites. “My sperm donor went split before I was born. But I have a wonderful step-dad, a hugely talented artist mom, and a half-sister who’s a pediatric nurse. All live in Chicago. I live in Seattle, but we’re close and see each other as often as we can.”

"I saw pictures." The capture and trial of Dwight Gus Treadwell had been national news for weeks. Images of Kendall and her family had been sent to Joe while the chopper was being prepped. Kendall alone on the witness stand, her scars still livid "They were all at the trial."

"Every day." Her fingers spread over the base of her throat "They knew what had happened of course. Julie took a leave of absence to take care of me for m-months afterwards."

She visibly pulled herself together, eyes distant, and rubbed her upper arms in a self-soothing motion he'd noticed earlier. "They sat right up front every day, all day. Stoic and unflinching. Then waited to get back to the hotel before they raced to the bathroom to throw up. It sickened me knowing how much my ordeal impacted them."

He wanted to hold her, but it wasn't his place. It felt goddamned wrong not to be able to comfort her. Hard as hell to remember she was an assignment. Strange that she felt like- *more.*

"Realistically," she said, making Joe speed up so as not to lose the gossamer tether. "How long do you estimate it'll take him to get here?"

"We started with six hundred miles between him and us," he told her. "Boise to Bozeman. In good weather. Ten hours if the roads were clear, maybe," he told her, stepping into an unoccupied bedroom. The king-sized bed, draped in red velvet, and accented with Christmas-themed pillows, looked decadently inviting.

The room smelled like ripe pears. Joe crossed to the bank of windows on the far wall. Really. He shouldn't be anywhere near a bed with this woman around. Bed? Hell. Who needed a bed? Any fairly flat surface would work. Not the damn point.

"He escaped from the infirmary late last night, or in the early hours this morning."

"He's encountering the same storm we are." Joe double checked the locks on both windows, and snugged the gap in the drapes. "The winds were estimated to hit seventy-five miles an hour in the last half hour. So he won't be moving fast. Plus he has to find transportation."

He didn't tell her that Treadwell had slashed the throats of two prison guards, killing both before he'd carjacked a guy on his way to work. Took his clothes as well. He, too, was dead.

Three people dead before Treadwell crossed into Mullan, Idaho at nine this morning. Another when he'd

switched vehicles at noon. All with Treadwell's signature. Albeit abbreviated MO with his fucking time restraints, he hadn't had time to toy with his victims as he'd done before his incarceration, he'd simply slashed their throats and moved on.

None of the latest had been redheaded females like his other victims. Like Treadwell's mother. He was no longer discriminating. He'd merely satisfied his blood-lust.

Kendall alone was his holy grail.

The weather would put a serious crimp in his travel plans, but Treadwell was determined enough, crazy enough, to persevere. The son of a bitch was proving he wouldn't give up.

Joe had given serious consideration to taking one of the snowmobiles and hiding out in one of the outlying guest cabins. Too close to the house he'd decided. But he knew of several holiday cabins on neighboring ranches fairly nearby.

Of course, *fairly* in these parts was twenty plus miles. And while no one would find her there, traveling those distances in this weather would prove dangerous, even life-threatening.

He might be able to stand the elements, although realistically, Joe knew even he wouldn't make it far or

fast. One thing was for sure. Kendall would never make it down the damned driveway in this weather. It was brutal out there. Even experienced ranchers and locals didn't brave the outdoors when it was this bad.

But the second the snow let up enough to take off, they'd be gone. If he could get the chopper up, he'd take her back to T-FLAC HQ. If he didn't think he'd make that fifty miles, he'd take her to the Dart's place twenty-five miles south of here. If the winds were still too high, he'd risk one of the snowmobiles. But get her away he would.

Because, despite the top-notch security in the house, his gut told him she wasn't safe here.

"I'm still willing to risk it, if you are." Kendall offered once again as if she were reading his mind. It was a disconcerting skill.

"Too dangerous." Joe brushed aside a strand of hair caught in her lashes, then let his fingers linger on her smooth cheek for just a second. It was a mistake. Because he didn't want to lightly touch this woman with victory scars on her body, and fear in her eyes.

He wanted to take her to bed and love her all night long. He wanted to wake up beside her in the morning and see her with sunlight on her face. He

wanted to be the one to permanently eradicate the fear in her eyes.

To paraphrase old Will Shakespeare, Joe thought facetiously, he was melting in his own fire. Too bad. He'd have to burn alone. Because the last thing this woman needed right now was his horny self. "Take a shower, then dress in layers. Do you have outside shoes suitable for this kind of weather?"

She nodded. "I doubt the water will be hot with the generator out."

"The tanks are well insulated. The water won't be hot, but it should still be warm."

#

Joe had accompanied her to the guest bedroom she'd commandeered while working night and day to "Christmas Supersize" the house for her client. The bed was made, but the room was cluttered. She'd brought a dozen boxes up to make more garlands, and there was faux greenery and red satin ribbons piled on top of boxes of lights and shiny ornaments.

The suite was beautifully decorated in shades of cream and a deep brick red and even had its own fragrant Christmas tree in the corner near the fireplace.

Not that Kendall cared about the décor or Christmas decorations at this point. The room had its

own luxurious en-suite bathroom, it also had a connecting door into an adjoining room. Three exits should she need one. The ordeal with Treadwell had taught her that – just as he'd taught her the true meaning of terror.

"Sorry about the mess." She shifted a large box out the way. "I've been working up here so I didn't have to haul everything for upstairs up the stairs. Almost done. The plan was to move to one of the guest cottages tomorrow to oversee the last minute party prep over the weekend once the caterers got here. Now that won't be necessary. I'll undecorate while I wait for the roads to be cleared, then fly back to Seattle."

She folded a lime green sweater she'd finished knitting this week, then stuffed it into a drawer. Not being able to sleep had its perks. She was able to accomplish a lot. But one full night's sleep would be amazing. Maybe one day.

"The room's lovely, but my insides are screaming go, go. go!" She put up her hand when Joe was about to speak. "I *know* we can't leave."

Damn it, she hated that her voice shook with the words. *Get a damn grip. Don't let Treadwell win.* He'd relish knowing she was terrified of him even when he was hundreds of miles away.

"I know, and *appreciate* that you're here to keep me safe." *Or as safe as you think you can*. "I know the house is secure. My rational brain knows all that, Joe. My lizard brain is screaming that I'm in mortal danger. I've spent months waking in a cold, clammy sweat, imagining Treadwell has found and kidnapped me again. Now he has.

He's out there. practically ringing the doorbell." Now she realized her calm was no more than a Band Aid over a gaping wound.

"I still can't make myself drive to the grocery store. I was taken on a Saturday morning, in full daylight, with people walking to and from their cars a hundred feet away. No one heard or saw a thing. Now I buy everything I need online"

She rubbed her upper arms. "I'm *sick* of living like this, damn it."

Joe's arrival, and the news he'd brought with him, stripped away the first feeling of peace she'd experienced in over a year.

She'd gone from enjoying the solitude, and the sheer joy of decorating such a large house for the holidays to a jolt back into the reality of her life with Treadwell still in it. Christmas used to be her favorite time of year, but the shine had gone off it after her

encounter with him. He'd sucked the light out of every aspect of her life for so long it was as if she'd had this gloomy cloud hovering directly over her head forfreaking*ever*.

It was a double whammy. News of Treadwell's escape, plus those-mind bending kisses from a man she'd only just met. Kendall's emotions were on overload. It didn't help that she was running on just a handful of hours of sleep.

Using his knee, Joe shoved a stack of boxes containing garlands out of his path, then came to stand in front of her. He looked even larger and more imposing up close. He didn't touch her, but God she wanted him to, and her body listed slightly toward him like metal filings to a magnet.

Kendall liked sex, not liked, *used* to like. Now she couldn't bear to be touched. Her shrink said that would pass. Having horny thoughts about Joe gave her hope. Not that she'd act on it, but it was nice to know it was possible.

"I hate that you're scared," he said quietly, "but in this instance, your fear will keep you sharp and focused. We're hardwired for self preservation, God only knows, you more so than most. It's natural that your fight or flight instincts are kicking in again. That's a good

thing. Courage isn't lack of fear. It's facing that fear head on, as you've been doing for the last fifteen months. You've already faced your worst-case scenario. Other than being on a remote Fijian island- which sounds damn appealing right about now- this place is as good as it gets for security."

Joe brushed her cheek with his finger, the touch featherlight, and yet Kendall felt it in her hair follicles. "Hell," he said, unaware that he'd sent all the atoms in her body careening around with nowhere to go. "*I'm* as good as it gets for security."

She believed him. He was big, intense and over-qualified for the job, and had built this magnificent house for his ex-wife to keep her safe while he was gone dealing with the worst people in the world.

"It's taken a year and a half to not freak out when someone touches me. And that's people I *know* touching me. That you were able to get close enough to kiss me-"

"Twice."

"*Twice.*" She smiled while her heart did backflips. It would be foolish to allow herself to fall for him just because he was big and strong, had built a house no one could breach, and kissed her like he really, really enjoyed it.

She’d never needed a hero, even though Joe seemed to have been custom tailored for the job, as if sent by Central Casting. It was dangerous to depend on anyone else. She’d saved herself from Treadwell once, and it was worth remembering that she might have to do that again.

“Remarkable,” she said softly. “Even more so, I liked being kissed by you."

He had darker blue dots in his irises, and close up his eyes were paler than she’d first thought. A true blue with no gray or green. Last year, right after the trial, to get away from the press, she and her sister had gone to Lefkas, Greece, an island in the Ionian Sea. Kendall had never seen such a clear, pure blue as the water there until she looked at Joe’s eyes close up.

"Liked?" Joe frowned, his palms running up and down her upper arms in a soothing gesture that when *he* did it, didn’t feel soothing at all. "Hmm. That's a pretty tepid review. Maybe we should try that again. They say third time's the charm."

A third kiss like the ones they'd shared downstairs would probably melt her thong.

Cupping her cheek, Joe trailed his lips over first one eyelid, then the other, guiding her body flush with

his with a light hand on the small of her back. Effervescent blood bubbled through her veins.

Was this feeling merely a natural attraction a woman felt for an attractive man? Or was she attracted to him because of what he represented?

Did it matter?

This was a moment out of time, not a lifetime commitment.

There wasn't a spare ounce of fat on him, and his chest felt rock hard where the softness of her breasts pressed against him. He was aroused, the thick length of his erection tantalizingly pressed against the juncture of her thighs. As his mouth found hers, moisture pooled between her legs and her nipples pebbled.

Cupping the back of her head, he tangled his fingers through her hair. His lips were firm and smooth as he learned the shape and taste of hers, taking his time. Kendall opened her mouth to his, leisurely never felt so good. He tasted a little like the cinnamon cookie he'd eaten earlier as he swept his agile tongue against hers.

God, the man knew how to kiss.

Eyes closed, she curled her arms around his neck, then stood on her toes for better access to his mouth so she could deepen the kiss. At five-nine, she wasn't used to a man towering over her. His large hands

moved down to cup her butt, drawing her even more tightly against him.

Kendall hummed her pleasure.

He deepened the kiss and for a few, blissful moments she forgot who he was and why he was here in the first place.

She felt the flexing of his muscles before he lifted his head. “Rain check?” Pupils dilated, he rubbed his slightly rough thumb across her damp bottom lip.

Kendall blinked away the sensual haze. “Right.” She dropped her arms and took a step back.

“You have time for a shower, it’ll unknot those muscles, and warm up your core. Dress in layers."

“In other words, be ready at a moment’s notice?”

“Yeah.” Joe lifted a curl of her hair from the front of her sweater and brought it to his nose. "They should bottle this smell.”

She smiled. “They do, it’s my shampoo.”

“I’m pretty sure it wouldn’t smell this great on anyone else. I'm going to the attic to set up the live surveillance feed from up there," he said, not missing a beat.

Kendall was more than a little tempted to ask if he would come into the bathroom while she showered so she wouldn’t be alone. But that would be turning her

power over to Treadwell on a silver platter and she refused to do that. She'd worked too hard – come too far to do that again.

God help her, she imagined Joe Zorn buck naked under the spray with her, which warmed her clear through.

Her emotions were all over the place. She had to focus and get her brain in gear. After he left her room, she tried her phone and was surprised to find an open line. She quickly speed-dialed Becky, her partner at Fait Accompli, who'd be at home in Seattle at this time of night.

"Call him your early Christmas present," Becky told her as soon as Kendall let her know Joe was with her. She only had two bars and the phone was crackly. Becky's voice faded in and out every time Kendall moved her head. "I've been -ing to call you since- cops called- this -rning at the crack of," Becky continued. "I even tried to book a flight out there to come and -ind you myself. Damn it. You scared the crap out of me w- -dn't reach -ou."

Kendall wasn't feeling too sanguine herself. Both body and brain were on sensory overload. She walked over to the window to see if the reception was any

better. Worse. She crossed the room to sit on the slipper chair at the dressing table.

"My friend Rick r -mended T-FLAC wh- -lled -ell Tre- escaped," Rebecca told her. Kendall turned her head slightly for better reception.

"How do *you* know a counterterrorist operative?"

". . .ister dated him years ago. Remember that hunky blond guy s--" The rest of her words were lost. Kendall vaguely remembered Becky's sister's ex-boyfriend.

"The manhunt," Becky's voice was suddenly shockingly clear. "Roadblocks yada, yada, yada are all over the news here. Despite the weather up your way, he's getting past all these damn people hunting for him.

A chill pebbled Kendall's skin.

"Every time that monster ditches a car, and hijacks another one, he *kills* someone. The press has been Johnny-on-the-spot with the lurid details. I hate to scare you even more, sweetie, but at last count he's killed seven people *today*. Trust this Joe guy with your life, Ken. Rick swears he's the best operative there is, and he'll guard you with his life."

Kendall let out a little murmur of panic. She hadn't known about the new killings, but she bet Joe had. She swallowed down nausea.

Sound calm. Be calm.

"The house is locked up like Fort Knox, and Joe has the biggest gun I've ever seen." There were a lot of other very big things about Joe Zorn. Fantasizing about him beat to hell being scared out of her mind. Besides, if Treadwell, in the unlikely event, and God forbid reached her, she owed it to herself to live life with joy as long as she could.

She'd decided in those first days after his awful, awful attack, life and death and all the degrees between were too unpredictable not to take the joy. Claim the good, as often as she could.

If tomorrow never came, she'd have the today she wanted – by her rules.

By her desires. By her wants and needs -no one else's.

"Don't let the guy with the big gun out of your sight," Becky warned unnecessarily. "On the plus side, if the local cops can't get to you, neither can Sick Bastard. But be careful until they have him in custody. Denise and I have already talked. I've cancelled the caterers, band and waitstaff. She's already taken care of the

guests. The roads are closed. Even the plows can't go out in that weather. And if they can't, Sick Bastard won't be on the roads either."

"It would've been a nice commission."

"I don't give a damn about the commission," her friend said fiercely. "I just want you safe. I'm glad this Joe guy's there with you so you aren't alone. Let him stick to you like glue until Treadwell is back in chains. Is back in a cage. Is somewhere far, far away from *you*. Promise me."

"Believe me," Kendall said dryly. "That's an easy promise to make." Joe had proved just how easily someone could take her gun away from her. So much for her false sense of confidence in her ability to protect herself.

"God, Beck, what if he *wasn't* here? What if I'd had no warning at all?"

"Well he is, and you *are* aware. They're going to catch him, and this damn time they'll lock him up and throw away the freaking key. And then you can stop living like a cloistered nun, and have your old life back."

Kendall didn't remember her old life. She no longer saw herself growing old after her ordeal. She didn't dare. Doing so, might create more fear for her to cope with. She believed she could die at any time and

understood that reality intimately. She knew her own mortality and would carry that with her for the rest of her life. She'd never allowed herself to imagine herself sitting in a rocking chair on the front porch, knitting or holding hands with a wonderful man, grandchildren scurrying around the yard.

She no longer dared hope for it- because Treadwell had taken away that dream, and it was too painful when trying to reconcile it with reality. It was more enjoyable to focus on Joe's body than it was to fixate on her killer closing in on her. Both thoughts made her blood pressure throb behind her eyeballs.

"I'm not saying I'm not terrified at the prospect of Treadwell showing up, but having Joe— " There was a pause on the other end of the line as her voice trailed off.

"And? But? If? And then?" Becky tried to finish the thought. "If you don't trust him to keep your ass safe, run like hell, lock him in somewhere, and find a place to hide."

"I trust he'll keep me safe from Treadwell," Kendall assured her. *But who's going to keep me safe from Joe Zorn?*

CHAPTER SIX

The powerful generator, housed in a fancy stone outbuilding located through the breezeway at the back of the house, *had* been crushed beyond repair. He and the builders hadn't anticipated this kind of snowfall during construction eleven years ago.

Fuck.

Joe went through the house making sure all the gas fireplaces were on. A six-thousand-square-foot open plan house was a bitch to heat at the best of times. When his ex had jumped at the idea of a log house, Joe had imagined a modest ranch house. But no. Denise had super-sized the damn thing until it was a fucking McMansion- made of logs. A bitch to heat and cool.

A separate generator, in a specially built room in the attic, powered all the security equipment. That was good, but that generator powered *only* the surveillance equipment. He'd reroute the dedicated Christmas lights generator to power some of the electricity in the most used rooms in the house.

A systems check from the attic indicated the fortified roof cameras were fully operational, the monitors inside picking up 360-degree real-time images. A blank wall of white. The motion sensor alarms and cameras would pick up the slightest movement in a mile radius. Exterior window and door alarms were now set for the lightest touch. Nothing larger than a rabbit could come within five thousand feet of the house without Joe receiving an alert on his phone.

Satisfied that no one could get into the house-unless Santa came down the non-working chimney of the gas fireplaces, they were in no danger of Treadwell showing up unannounced.

He headed back downstairs, hoping Kendall was done with her shower, and fully dressed. Including shoes, because he found her pale, naked feet unbearably sexy.

Joe's mind conjured assorted salacious images and improbable scenarios.

The bedroom became marginally brighter with the addition of the lamp he carried. After placing it on the dressing table, he crossed to sit in one of the extra-wide easy chairs flanking the stone-faced gas fireplace.

He *liked* women. He particularly enjoyed attractive, intelligent women. Kendall Metcalf was both. In spades. So his heightened physical attraction to her didn't come as a surprise. The woman's sex appeal was off the charts.

Stretching out his long legs toward the fire, Joe rested his Heckler & Koch double action pistol on the chair arm beside him. He wasn't a guy who spent a hell of a lot of time contemplating his own navel, but his visceral reaction to her was as intriguing as it was puzzling. He ignored the distraction of picturing a wet, naked, Kendall as he heard the shower running.

Joe tried to pinpoint exactly *what* he felt when he was with her. The high lust factor was a given. But it was the strange, unfamiliar feeling in his chest that had him mystified.

A. . . flutter? An extra heartbeat?
Something wholly alien. He hadn't felt this way about Denise. Which was probably why, five months after saying their vows, their marriage ended- with a fizzle- in divorce. That had been almost eleven years ago.

Clearly Denise had felt that alien *something* for Adam Cameron. They had two kids, another on the way, and appeared to be as in love now as they had been when Adam had rushed the ex Mrs. Zorn to the altar

three months after the ink was dry on her divorce papers.

Joe was happy for them. He liked them both. He hadn't been heartbroken at the end of his marriage. He thought he should've been, but he wasn't. Every now and then he wondered, on a purely academic level, exactly what that elusive *something* factor *was* that the couple had. He'd never found it for himself.

Denise called it spark, magic and lots of other female words that until a few hours ago, he'd pretty much dismissed as the rantings of a romantic.

Spark was a pretty damned good description for the sensations currently annoying him. Why Kendall Metcalf? Why now? He should be thinking about guns, ammo, close combat, points of entry, instead his mind conjured all sorts of enticing images of his protectee.

Sparks, he decided, were distracting as hell.

Without making a conscious decision, Joe had created this nomadic lifestyle. Well, not created it so much as fallen into it without much objection.

In his experience, nothing good ever came of analyzing one's choices. He shook his head at musings brought on by flickering firelight and thoughts of a wet, naked Kendall in the other room.

"Get a grip," he told himself firmly.

From his vantage point he could keep an eye on all the doors in the room. He didn't like sitting here waiting like this. He was a man of action. But Mother Nature wasn't cooperating. If he had backup he'd go outside and check the perimeter. But he wouldn't take Kendall out there. No matter how secure the house he wouldn't leave her there alone.

It would suit him perfectly if that son of a bitch Dwight Treadwell did one right thing in his miserable sick life; walked in now. One shot between the bastard's eyes and it would be over.

Silva had sent Joe the court transcripts along with copies of a dozen newspaper articles which he'd scanned while the ground crew readied the chopper. Hell, was that just a few hours ago?

He'd been sickened by what Kendall had endured at the hands of that psychopath. He'd also felt the ticking of the time bomb, knowing that while he was en route to her, Treadwell was too. At the time Treadwell had kidnapped and tortured Kendall, it was confirmed he'd brutalized, then killed five other women. At his arraignment that number had jumped horrifically to twenty-three.

Kendall was Treadwell's only living victim, the one person left to identify the son-of-a-bitch in court.

Which, according to the transcripts Joe had read, she'd done. Clearly and succinctly, with Treadwell sitting right there in front of her.

Her attention to detail and minutia in her event planning business had served her well. She'd recalled in stark, no-nonsense language details that only one of his victims could possibly know. She'd given a specific and concise physical description of the man. And she'd gone into clinical, precise detail about what she'd endured for almost seventy-two hours at Treadwell's hands, the reading of which had turned Joe's stomach.

What she'd suffered, and the retelling of it, had taken unimaginable guts. Joe had a clear picture of what made up the mental characteristic of the serial killer. He'd also understood the subtext in Kendall's testimony. The Evil Prick had played with her like a cat with a half dead mouse. He'd slashed her deep and he'd slashed her shallow, letting her suffer as he taunted her with death, but kept her alive. Barely.

Treadwell had kept her holed up in a trailer deep in the woods south of Seattle for three days. In all that time, she hadn't known just how fucking close she was to civilization.

Considering the timeline, the slash across her throat must've still been raw and livid as she sat in court

facing her attacker. The jury had deliberated for all of forty-seven minutes - including a bathroom break - before coming back with a guilty verdict on all counts.

Washington was one of thirty-eight states with the death penalty. But Treadwell's attorneys had managed to get a sentencing recommendation of life without parole after the verdict in exchange for the killer's cooperation in finding the bodies of the other twenty-three victims.

Treadwell had received twenty-three consecutive life sentences, plus one concurrent sentence, for the attempted first degree on Kendall and another seventy-five years for her torture. He'd also vowed, before the court, that he would one day find Kendall Metcalf and finish the job he'd started. And the next time she wouldn't get away.

And yet despite all that, he'd somehow managed to escape while being transported between one facility and another after he'd sliced, diced and fucking killed two inmates a few weeks earlier. Joe suspected soon after Treadwell had read the reports of Kendall's whereabouts.

He'd know he'd be transported to a maximum-security facility. He'd know if he was going to escape it had to be while in transit.

Hell, if it were up to Joe, Treadwell would be drawn and quartered, dropped down a hole and left to rot slowly and painfully. An eye for an eye.

The shower turned off and he glanced up just in time to see, through the partially open door, a flash of pale hip and leg as Kendall reached for a towel.

It was going to be a long night.

Deck the Halls played softly on the emergency radio sitting on the dresser as Kendall emerged from the bathroom, blotting her hair dry. A towel in one hand, and carrying a second lantern in the other. She brought with her the heady fragrance of fresh pears on a cloud of steam.

She looked deliciously touchable with her still damp, pink cheeks, shining eyes and dewy velvety skin. She placed the lantern beside the one on the dresser, and used both hands to blot her hair. The lanterns flickered with her movements. Her feet were still bare, but thank God she was dressed. Jeans and an oversized purple sweater with the words;

☐ Naughty.
☐ Nice.
☑ I Tried.

He indicated her sweater. "One of your creations?" *If you knew how badly I want you, sweetheart, you'd run like hell.*

"It is, would you like me to knit a sweater for you?" she asked, sweetly oblivious to how desirable she looked in the golden lamplight. "What color would you like? Blue to match your eyes?"

With the muted glow of the oil lamp, the rumpled bed behind him, and the flicker of the fireplace, the ambiance was a little too romantic and seductive for his peace of mind. Especially now that he knew what she tasted like. "I don't want people reading my chest when I'm on an op."

She smiled as he'd meant her to do. "No words then." The smile slipped from her lips, and she watched him with big, serious eyes. "Will you have sex with me?"

Joe blinked at the non sequitur. "Say what?" He heard her just fine, it was computing the request that was hard to wrap his mind around, since he'd been thinking the same damn thing.

Dusty rose bloomed in her cheeks. "I know we just met, and, believe me, this is a once in a lifetime offer. But I'm feeling my mortality tonight. He's out there and getting closer. I need to at least feel alive for a couple of hours before he shows up."

She was optimistic, hell, he wouldn't last a couple of *minutes* if he were inside her right now. "No." It came out a hell of a lot more harshly than he intended. There was no getting away from the fact that he wanted her. God only knew, what man wouldn't? She was gorgeous, smart, funny and sexy as hell. But he sure as shit wasn't going to act on it. Not tonight anyway.

Dropping down on the foot of the bed, she let out a shaky breath. Her eyes were clear and penetrating as she asked, "Is it the one-night stand aspect? Do the scars repulse you? You're not attracted to me?" she said, all in one breath. "We can do it in the dark. It's just sex, Joe. Not a lifetime commitment."

"I *am* attracted to you." Joe admired her straightforwardness. He admired a hell of a lot of other things, like the fact that he could see she wasn't wearing a bra under the purple sweater. He'd like to peel- *Hey! Up here, pal!*

"I don't give a shit about your scars other than the pain they caused you, and when we make love it will be with all the lights on. No secrets. But this is neither the time nor the place."

"I think this is the perfect time and place," she told him, hopping off the foot of the bed. "Quick, energetic sex. No strings. No regrets. We wouldn't even

have to exchange phone numbers. We've already proved we'd be compatible in bed if those kisses are any indication."

Already disconcerted by his strong physical attraction to her, Joe wasn't about to debate her. "I can either sit here and watch over you as you sleep, or I can station myself outside the door," he said roughly, trying to ignore the gentle sway of her unfettered breasts and the way the firelight painted her in shades of amber.

"Your call. I'm here to protect you, remember? The second this snow lets up, I'll wake you, and we'll be outta here. But until then I'm on duty, and won't be sleeping."

"Okay." She met his gaze with a level look. "Under the circumstances, I doubt if I'll sleep either. But to be honest, without a solid five hours sleep, I tend to not function on all cylinders. So, I'd like to at least try to get a few hours in before we leave. I'd feel a lot safer if you were beside me. I don't mind if you want to leave the lantern on all night. I'd just want. . . ."

Protection. "Company?"

She walked over to the window, leaving the scent of fresh pears in her slipstream. "I need to sleep, but I'm too keyed up."

"There's a gym in the basement." Joe wished to hell she'd land somewhere. All the pacing was making him dizzy. Or was it the clean soapy fragrance of her as she passed him? Or her bra-less state? Or her bare feet- damn it to hell, he was becoming quite attached to her bare, endearingly too large, feet. Joe felt a sharp stab in his belly that was neither pain nor pleasure as she did another circuit of the room.

With a shake of her head, Kendall opened the door to the armoire which held a mini refrigerator which no doubt still held its temperature and removed a bottle of sweet tea. She held it up. He shook his head. After pouring herself a glass, she resumed pacing, sipping as she walked.

She stopped to run a hand through her still damp hair. It was the deep, rich orangey-red of an excellent Hennessy cognac. Joe loved a mellow brandy on a cold winter's night.

"Not to feel alone tonight. That's what I really meant to say, instead of sex." She gave him an assessing look. "Honestly I haven't been able to stand having anyone touch me in a year and a half. So despite my offer, and in spite of how hot you are, sex would be a mistake for me right now anyway. Thank God one of us is thinking straight."

She took another sip of cold tea, concentrating on the liquid she was swirling in her glass. Joe wondered if the woman ever relaxed. Hell. If she *could* relax. Filled with nervous energy she eventually came to perch on the edge of the other chair near the fire.

Wired and ready to blow she twisted the stem of her glass between her fingers, then looked up to meet his eyes. "I've worked my ass off to overcome this knee-jerk reaction every time I hear something behind me. A creak when the house settles, positive every metallic glint I see is a knife."

Her gaze was steady as she looked at him. "I don't want Treadwell to win, Joe. I don't want to live in fear for the rest of my life because of what he did to me. I thought I'd done pretty well up until now. But knowing he's somewhere out there. Knowing that I'm no longer a random victim to him, but someone he *specifically* wants to kill terrifies me."

She hugged herself. "Before I didn't know what to expect. Now I do."

"He won't come within shouting distance of you, honey." Joe kept his voice low and soothing, his gaze away from the frightened, erratic pulse of her heartbeat in her slender white throat. And that scar. Fuck.

"Whether we stay or go, I won’t let you out of my sight for the duration. That's a promise.

CHAPTER SEVEN

Kendall's heart throbbed erratically at her boldness, and her stomach twisted with the rejection, even though he was right. Her skin prickled sweaty and hot. She didn't blame him. For God's sake, they'd known each other for all of a minute. He must think she was a nutcase.

"Hey, don't worry about it," she told him brightly. "You'll be sitting right there keeping guard while I sleep, right?"

"Kendall-" he whispered.

She lifted her chin.

His gaze flickered to her throat- the scar- then came back up to meet hers. All she read there was pity. An emotion she'd seen more times than she cared to remember. Thanks to Treadwell, she'd forever be *The Surviving Victim.*

Little else seemed to matter to people.

She almost remembered a time when people looked upon her with acknowledgement – praise even – for the way she'd picked herself up after the court ordeal. She'd made a life for herself – defined that life. And now that was gone.

"It's late and I'm three stages beyond exhausted," she inserted around a genuine yawn. After all, what man would want to put his mouth anywhere near the red, welt of a scar? It was a painful truth, one she wasn't sure she'd ever get used to. She added that to her mental list of reasons for wanting Treadwell to burn in hell.

She yawned again. "Wake me when it's time to leave, okay?"

The tremor she'd been battling since Joe had told her about Treadwell's escape intensified as she walked across the room to the high, king-

sized bed. Why was she mad at him? They didn't *know* one another. He'd kissed her. No big deal.

She tossed the decorator pillows onto the floor with a little more gusto than was warranted, then pulled back the terracotta-colored velvet spread with hands that shook a little.

Fully dressed, she climbed under the covers, lay on her side and curled into a ball. Her fingers went to her neck. The scar always throbbed when she thought about that night.

She usually slept naked. Now, with damp hair, and twisty clothes, she was uncomfortable. She also felt antsy, annoyed, and sorry for herself, all of which pissed her off. She didn't know who she was madder at; Treadwell for creeping back into her life like the rodent he was, or Joe for tempting her, but not being tempted enough *by* her, or herself for- she didn't know for *what*—which annoyed her even more.

As tired as she was, now she couldn't freaking sleep. She lay still. Not moving, not twitching, not showing Joe that she was awake. That lasted oh, sixty seconds. She had to straighten the sweater that was riding up uncomfortably. Then her leg itched. . .

The room was warm, but she burrowed under the blankets anyway. Blocking out the flickering light. And Joe. She wanted to bury her head like an ostrich. The problem was, when she came up for air, the situation would be exactly the same.

She tried to concentrate on just how damn, *freaking* uncomfortable she was trying to sleep in her clothes. There were only two other subjects to mull over, ponder, dissect, and agonize about. Joe. Or Treadwell.

One aggravated her, but made her feel protected. The other downright terrified her and

made her painfully aware of how vulnerable she was.

Would she ever believe herself completely safe? God, she hoped so. She'd done every single thing her therapist had told her to do. She'd taken self defense classes, bought a gun, made sure she knew how to use it, and when to use it. She was still faithfully going to therapy.

A violent criminal victimization is a real-life classical conditioning experience in which being attacked is an unconditioned stimulus that produces unconditioned responses of fear, anxiety, terror, helplessness, pain, and other negative emotions. Any stimuli that are present during the attack are paired with the attack and become conditioned stimuli capable of producing conditioned responses of fear, anxiety, terror, helplessness, and other negative emotions.

Intellectually she knew she'd be in a much better position to defend herself. *This* time. But

her body was reacting as though she were once again in danger. Her teeth began chattering. How could she be sweating and cold at the same time? A sob broke through the tight constriction of her throat and tears scalded her cheeks as she curled into a fetal position, and hugged herself.

Oh, God. She was so *tired* of being afraid.

Unexpectedly, the mattress dipped, and Joe started to gently towel dry her hair.

She put up a hand when he touched her head.

"No, stay put, I've got this." Slowly her muscles relaxed as he massaged her scalp with sure hands. "Close your eyes, I've got you."

CHAPTER EIGHT

"Will you sleep?" she asked lazily when her hair was towel dried to his satisfaction.

Joe reached over and repositioned his gun on the bedside table beside him, then swung his legs up on the mattress with his back supported by the headboard.

Kendall shifted under the covers until she found the perfect spot to rest her cheek in the curve of his shoulder. Joe glided his hand under the sweater to rub her back in slow, lazy circles and her muscles relaxed as she hovered close to sleep.

It seemed she'd just closed her eyes, but she woke with a scream and bolted upright in bed. Disoriented and shaking she looked around the dimly lit bedroom as if she'd never seen it before.

Beside her Joe said softly. "Bad dream?"

Eyes dark and haunted, she nodded, making her hair slide over her shoulders. "He's out there."

"No, he's not," he said with conviction. "Come here, sweetheart." He pulled her back into his arms.

"Silva gave us an update not an hour ago, remember? He's stuck in Boise. That's seven hours away on a good day. And that's only if he manages to commandeer another vehicle. If the storm lets up. If he isn't stopped by one of the roadblocks between here and there. Everyone is looking for the son of a bitch, honey. He won't get anywhere near you. I promise."

"He doesn't have to be anywhere near me to scare me spitless," Kendall said tightly.

#

She was shivering hard now. Joe tightened his arms around her and rubbed her back in long soothing strokes. Her bare skin felt warm and silky smooth.

Except for the raised keloids from nape to waist.

Fucking, fucking hell.

"How did you get away that night?" he asked, tightening his arm around her. He knew of course. It had been in the transcripts. But he wanted her to remember taking action. To remember that in the end, she hadn't been helpless.

"I'd lost track of time. There was tinfoil over the windows, and I had no idea if it was day or night. Or how long he'd h-had me. He kept me chained to the handle of the oven. There was- b-blood all over me."

Shit. Bad idea. "But you managed to outsmart the sick fu-bastard and get away, didn’t you?" His own stomach lurched at the thought of the cuts on her body and how terrified she must’ve been.

“When the first scalpel slipped out of his hand onto the floor, he was livid and showed his anger by kicking me in the ribs. When he left the kitchen, I toed it farther under the stove. I knew I wouldn’t last another round. That was the first time he’d lost his cool and it scared me spitless. For days he’d been cold, detached, clinical. He wasn’t just mad he’d dropped it, he was enraged and let me know it was all my fault.

“He came back, the clean scalpel in his hand, and said: ‘I’ve enjoyed our time together, Kendall’ and took a key out of his pocket. I thought- Oh, God. He’s going to kill me now."

She was breathing fast, and Joe stroked her back, listening to her erratic breathing. Fury blazed in his belly as she talked.

"But he opened the padlock on the chain, then showed me the clean shiny scalpel in the other hand, and hoisted me up off the floor by my hair. He needed me standing. He wanted to add my blood to his wall of s-splatter."

Christ.

"He considered himself an artist," she said without inflection. "I was his medium. He told me. . .told me that I had to be positioned just right so that when he sliced my artery, the spray of blood would add to the mural he'd been creating on the-the wall of the trailer."

The mural that had the blood of dozens of other women dried on it. A challenge for the forensic teams to unravel the DNA. "Jesus, sweetheart. I'm sorry. So sorry. But you beat him at his own game. You got away."

"I slid the scalpel out with my foot. While he angled me for best effect, then started to cut m-my throat, despite considerable blood loss, I managed to plunge the first scalpel up under his chin. I didn't have enough energy to stab it right into his jugular, but I cut him badly enough that he shrieked with shock and fell to his knees clutching his bleeding jaw. Then I ran for my life. When I finally got to a road, I saw the lights of a track development barely a mile away." She rubbed her upper arms. "Someone could have heard me screaming. No one came."

When a passing motorist had almost driven over her, he'd called 911 about the naked dead body sprawled in the middle of the road. The Good Samaritan had, thank God, made the call, but Kendall had almost

bled out because the man had stayed in his vehicle until the cops arrived.

"Yes," she burrowed tightly against him, shaking hard enough to shatter. "I got away."

At what cost? Joe thought, wrapping her in his arms and holding her tightly. Damn. He hated that he was in a hurry-up-and-wait position. He didn't like not having options. He had a fantasy of getting Kendall to safety, then returning to the house to wait for Treadwell himself. One on one.

Before the cops arrived and made a nice, polite arrest, Joe wanted just half an hour with the son of a bitch – breaking every bone in his body. Just long enough to give Dwight Treadwell the punishment he so richly deserved.

He listened to the storm die down beyond the sealed windows and checked the safety on the H&K as Kendall slept half sprawled over his body. She needed the rest, and it felt damn good having her in his arms, her warm breath moist against his throat.

CHAPTER NINE

The snow had stopped an hour ago, and the winds had died down. While Kendall slept, Joe went downstairs to check that the motion sensors were still operational, and made sure the strategically positioned exterior cameras were still clear of snow. All good.

While he'd always trusted his instincts and gut feelings, *this* itch on the back of his neck was illogical.

He, better than anyone else, knew the house was impenetrable. As long as they stayed inside, she'd be safe.

Still, Joe felt an illogical urgency to get out of the house like a clawing entity inside him.

The sat phone buzzed in his back pocket as he started going upstairs.

"Feebs *and* cops en route. ETA fifty minutes," Silva told him. "Be advised. Treadwell in the wind."

And there he had it. *Fuck.*

On the landing, half way up, he looked out of the high, arched window at the view of the backyard. The perimeter security lights showed a small snow hill. The location of the chopper. Not good.

Would the damn thing start when they were ready to leave? Even though the storm was easing up and the winds had calmed, some, could it be flown in this weather? He'd been advised not to even try. *Fuck that*.

Hoofing it was out.

The snowmobiles in the garage were a possibility, but the weather was still too iffy to chance it. A snow plow would work, but it was slow as hell, and how far would he have to travel to even get his hands on one?

"What's the matter," Kendall asked when he returned to the bedroom. She was up and wore socks, no shoes. Twisting her thick hair into a skein, she pinned it to the back of her head.

The ninety minutes of sleep had pinked her cheeks and brightened her eyes.

"Other than the weather. The uncertainty. And a serial killer?"

"The good news is it stopped snowing and blowing about an hour ago. Snow plows are already out clearing main roads and the FBI will be here in about an hour. Bad; Treadwell managed to elude my eye in the sky. The helicopter is covered in a thick blanket of snow. When the Feebs get here, I'll go out and see what condition it's in and if it can be flown. If it is, we'll head out to T-FLAC headquarters right away. It's only fifty-four miles away."

A location impossible to find. Even if a person knew of its existence.

"Why go anywhere? A gnat can't get inside the house. We stay put until they catch him, right?"

"I like options. Ready to go down? Grab your shoes."

"Downstairs," she told him on the way. "Hang on." Kendall had left a pair of bright blue, fur-lined, knee-high boots in the hall closet, and plopped herself down on the area rug to pull them on.

Joe held out his hand to pull her up when she was done. "Man. I'd give a year's pay to see you in those- and nothing else."

"Yeah?" Her smile didn't quite reach her eyes as she came up beside him in a smooth move he had to admire. "That can be arranged."

"I'll consider that a promise and take a rain check."

He put his arm around her shoulders and gave her a squeeze. He knew she was scared, and he wasn't going to diminish that emotion by pretending he wasn't aware of her feelings. As much as he sympathized, her fear would keep her on her toes.

He should be feeling a mild form of relief at this point. The storm had relented enough for them to leave. He had ample backup, the means to leave quickly, and there had been no reported sightings of Treadwell for almost five hours.

Instead Joe felt a tightening at the back of his neck.

Something was off. There was the sense- Fuck it- the *anticipation*- of impending danger.

He'd been a counterterrorist operative for fifteen years and trusted his gut.

Treadwell was close. Too close.

"Want a cookie? Neither do I," she tossed the one she held back onto the animal plate as she passed. "No hot coffee," she told him brightly as she opened the dark

refrigerator. "I can make another pot for that all important caffeine jolt. Or a Coke?"

"Pass."

He snagged her arm as she passed, drawing her against him to cup her cheek. Her skin felt cold despite the warmth of the house.

"In an hour or less," he promised her, "I'll have you back in a warm bed. With a very hot me." Joe brushed his mouth over hers. And then because, honest to God, he couldn't keep his body parts off her body parts, pulled her tightly into his arms and crushed his mouth down on hers.

The kiss was short but filled with promise. Joe lifted his head, then went back in to rub his nose on hers in an Eskimo kiss. "This'll be a hell of a story to tell our grandkids over the campfire, won't it?"

Her pretty eyes narrowed. "I hate camping."

"You're young. Plenty of time to learn to love it. Kids like that sort of thing."

Someone pounded on the door, making her freeze like a startled deer.

"Easy, sweetheart," he told her calmly. "The cavalry, remember?" It was just after seven a.m., and still dark outside. "Almost over. Got your gun?"

When she patted a pocket, he smiled. "I'll let them in. We'll have our own personal army to accompany us to the chopper. And when he gets here, the local cops and the Feds will be here to welcome him."

Kendall wrapped a blue and yellow striped knit scarf around her throat several times. The thing was a mile long. "From your lips to God's ear." She fished a pair of child-sized blue gloves from a pocket and pushed her hands into them. Strangely they fit.

The pounding came again, urgent and impatient.

Joe looked at the display on his watch, slid the screen to get a view from the camera outside the front door. He recognized the three men, bulky in their heavy outerwear.

"The local cops made it here first," he told her. Joe knew the bundled up, boot-stomping officers. "I know these guys. Go to the kitchen while I let them in."

She'd dug a blue knit, fur lined hat out of a pocket, and pulled it on over her head with both hands. It covered her ears and forehead.

She looked adorable. He couldn't resist and dropped another quick, hard kiss to her mouth. "Scoot." He waited until she was well into the kitchen and out of sight.

He wouldn't risk taking a single chance. With the H&K in plain view, he opened the front door.

Joe let the three guys in, glimpsing the snowplow parked near the steps out front. He raised a brow. "You came on a *plow*?"

The door slammed shut with the force of the wind behind the last man. The wind might have died down, but it was far from over. Clearly the men hadn't been able to drive a regular vehicle through the snow banks. Damn it to hell.

"It was that or *follow* the snow plow. We cut out the middleman." Chief of police, red-faced, William 'Buckeye' Wilder said as he slapped a beefy hand on his back. "Good to see you, son."

Joe accepted the hearty slap with a smile. Buckeye's son had played football with Joe at the U of Montana way back when. *Go Grizzlies*. "This time last year." They'd all attended Denise and Adam's last annual Christmas extravaganza.

Todd McKenzie grinned. "You stuck it out for a whole two hours."

Joe shrugged. "Had to get back to work." Preferred batching it at HQ where it was at least quiet. It was the shits to feel lonely in that big a crowd. "Miss Metcalf's in the kitchen. I'll introduce you, then I want to

go out and check on the chopper. You heard Treadwell's in the wind?"

"Yeah. The local FBI field office let us know. They're sending a guy."

At his all clear, Kendall came out of the kitchen. Joe introduced her to the men.

"Y'all are gonna fly a copter outta here?" Buckeye asked Joe after touching his Stetson briefly to Kendall. "Wouldn't suggest it, son," he said grimly. "Know you've been flyin' since you was yae tall, and that wind mighta wound down, but it's still high enough to bring you down before you lift off."

Joe suspected he was right, but he'd done more than fly over the Montana landscape in the last ten years. He had infinite confidence in his own abilities as a pilot, but until he went out there, and saw for himself exactly how bad it was, he wasn't going to negate their best, most expedient form of transportation.

"Could be," was all he said. He glanced from man to man. "Is there any other way? All I saw out there was a snowplow. Not exactly my idea of a speedy getaway."

"Better to wait four or five hours, and take a couple of the Cameron's snowmobiles when the wind lets up a bit more." Sonny Goodwin, a younger brother

of another of Joe's college buddies suggested, stomping the snow off his boots onto the hall rug. "Don't suppose there's any hot coffee around?" he asked hopefully.

"I was just about to put a pot on." Kendall looked at Joe with a frown. "What are our options?"

Not many, Joe thought with frustration. A plodding snowmobile a child on a tricycle could follow, or the chopper currently buried under several feet of snow. But hanging around for another four or five hours didn't feel like an option. No one could get inside.

"Stay here while I check the chopper. We'll take it from there."

"I'll come with you."

He touched her cheek with his fingertips. "No need for both of us to freeze our asses off unless it's necessary. We all need hot coffee. Sonny, go help Miss Kendall. I'll be back in ASAP."

If the chopper could be cleared of several feet of snow, he'd start it, lift off, and bring it back to land on the front lawn. If not he'd go to plan B. Whatever the fuck that was. One thing at a time.

He headed for the door, pulling on his gloves. He turned around with his hand on the door handle.

"Do not," he said to the men, "I repeat. Do *not* let her out of your sight for even a second. Treadwell is out

there. I can feel the son of a bitch breathing down our necks. Lock the door behind me. I should be back before the Feebs get here."

With a last glance at Kendall, Joe opened the front door letting in a blast of frigid air.

"Be careful," she told him.

Joe nodded, his eyes holding hers. Then he let the door slam shut behind him.

#

"Well," Kendall said brightly as the men trooped into the kitchen with her, making some of the lanterns flare. "Coffee it is."

The men trailed her like ants on their way to a picnic, their movement causing the lanterns to flicker. The baking sheets of cookies and the two red mugs she and Joe had used last night, still sat on the center island. Kendall carried the dirty dishes to the sink.

She felt like an overwound watch. Kendall didn't want to be here without Joe. It didn't matter that she had these three guys in his place. Three average law enforcement officers didn't equal one Joe Zorn.

She felt what Joe felt- imminent danger. What if Treadwell was out there waiting, and he hurt Joe-

What if- What if. Beneath the scarf wound about her throat, the scar seemed to pulse. Oh, God. . .

"Help yourselves to those cookies. I'll get the coffee going." She picked up the flashlight on the counter. "Were there any vehicles on the road?"

"No ma'am. Nobody and nothin' out there for miles. We know Treadwell's reputation. The whole county has been warned and is on alert. Even if they could get out, no one will until he's been apprehended. They know all about him, don't worry."

"Nobody who hasn't felt his knife at their throat really knows about Treadwell," Kendall told them bitterly as she spooned coffee grounds into the basket. "If you guys made it to the ranch, so can he."

She disappeared into the pantry/safe room wanting to lock the door, and hide in there until Joe got back, but a tall, beanpole of a guy with sandy hair, and sympathetic eyes followed her inside.

"You know Joe's a counterterrorist operative, right, ma'am?" Sonny blocked the door. "Used to be a Marine. He's the baddest ass – Excuse my French- out there. He and my brother Ryan went to school together, and they both joined T-FLAC right outta college. Ryan doesn't say much – Them fighting terrorists and all, but he says Zorn's one hardass son of a bitch, and *no one* messes with him. One bad dude isn't going to get the best of Joe, I promise. You've got nothing to be worried

about. And me and the others are here while Joe's out there checking on the helicopter."

"Thanks, Sonny."

Coats were removed, and guns exposed while Kendall pot the coffee pot on the burner. "Did you all know Joe when he lived here with Denise?" she asked, as she took down mugs.

"His folks owned the ranch, he got it when they passed. Joe wanted to give Miss Denise whatever she wanted." His smile showed a crooked eye tooth. “She wanted a lot. Joe would’a been happy with the old cabin his dad had right on this here spot. But he built the big house for her. And as it turned out for her and Adam.

The radio suddenly came on in the other room. *I’m Dreaming of a White Christmas* belted out.

"Power’s back on," one of the younger officers said.

The older man smacked the back of his head. "Does it *look* like the power’s back on, Morgan?"

"It’s the emergency radio," Kendall told them absently.

Music to be scared by. Great. Just what she needed.

The men polished off most of the cookies as the coffee started to perk, filling the kitchen with the rich

fragrance of expensive beans. She was so not in the Christmas spirit. The house smelled of Christmas. It looked like Christmas. But, oh God, it didn't feel like a joyous time of the year at all. She was scared.

Scared for herself because she knew her killer was close.

Scared out of her mind for Joe who was out there alone.

Was he okay?

Of course he was.

He had to be.

Kendall drank the too strong coffee just to feel the heat of it going down.

He knew what he was doing. He also knew the area very well. She gulped down half her coffee before she realized she'd added neither creamer nor Sweet 'n Low.

The annoying song, *Grandma Got Run Over By a Reindeer* blasted from the other room jangling her nerves even more. She set her mug down with a little more force than necessary.

"Getting on your last nerve, is it, ma'am?" The younger blonde officer asked, his eyes twinkling with amusement, or sympathy, or blast it - probably no

feelings one way or the other at all. "Want for me to go turn it off?"

Kendall gave him a smile. "Just *down* would help, thanks." She glanced at her watch. Joe had been gone for less than half an hour. It felt like an eternity.

No it didn't. She knew what an eternity felt like.

She'd experienced a time without end in that single-wide trailer in the woods fifteen months ago. *That* was eternity.

The officer took a cookie to go and ambled off in the direction of the great room. There was really nothing to say to the men in the kitchen with her and the silence stretched, helped only marginally by a rousing rendition of *Jingle Bell Rock.*

She had just refilled her mug when a loud crack sounded from outside. The retort was as loud as a gunshot. With a scream, she jolted, spilling scalding coffee down her front.

The two younger men drew their guns in the blink of an eye.

The older man went to the window to peek through the blinds, then turned back to the others. "Stand down. Tree split in half. We're seeing plenty in this weather."

As the men holstered their weapons Kendall felt lightheaded and sick to her stomach. God, she wanted this to be over.

"You okay, ma'am?"

She nodded jerkily. Her midriff stung from contact with the hot coffee which had soaked into her thick sweater. "I'll just go and rinse this off." She didn't want to go upstairs, instead she grabbed the heavy, optimistic-yellow, down coat slung over a chair back in case she needed to strip off the sweater.

"I'll go with you." Sonny offered. He looked spooked, too, which didn't fill her with confidence.

She needed just a few minutes to compose herself, give herself a pep talk. Hell. Talk herself off the ceiling. Her heart was still racing.

"The bathroom door is right there," she pointed down a short hallway to show the door was visible from where they stood. "There's no window, I'll be safe in there for a few minutes."

She took one of the flashlights off the kitchen counter, went into the powder room and shut the door behind her. The room was decadently large. It had looked charming a couple of days ago when she'd placed red votive candles amidst clusters of holly berries

and glossy green leaves between the rocks of a small fountain on the counter. Right now it just looked – dark.

She pulled her sweater over her head. The sting of the faint red mark across her middle was already fading. She let herself look at the scars Treadwell had made on her body. Those too were fading. Much faster than those he'd made to her psyche.

As the light from the flashlight dimmed, indicating- damn it to hell- that it needed new batteries, she glanced in the mirror over the vanity and gave a choked, semi-hysterical laugh. Even though she'd pinned up her hair, it was already coming loose, drying every which way, making her look like a wild woman. And even in the flickering light, her skin appeared pale. Fear did that to a girl.

She took a deep, shuddering breath, held it, and exhaled slowly. And again.

Better.

A loud *bambambam* on the front door stopped her heart.

A few seconds later one of the guys shouted, "It's the FBI guy, Miss Kendall!"

She should feel better with an army here to protect her. But the only one she trusted was still outside. "Give him a cup of coffee, I'll be a few minutes."

Because any second now the flashlight was going to plunge her into blackness. At least there were men in the bright kitchen to dispel her irrational fear.

Treadwell couldn't get inside the house. He couldn't stand outside and huff and puff and blow the house down. If he was here at all. Even the FBI guy had taken longer than the cops, and he'd come from a local field office. Last she'd heard Treadwell was five hours away. And even if he wasn't—

He. Could. Not. Get. Into. The. House.

He couldn't get past law enforcement officers trained to shoot to kill.

He wouldn't get past Joe.

Kendall let out a shaky breath as she pulled the sweater over her head. Her bra was wet, but she left it on as she rinsed the coffee out of the heavy garment, then blotted it with a towel. Closing the lid on the toilet, she sat down, not ready to face a bunch of strange guys all looking at her trying to imagine what Treadwell had done to her.

The flashlight dimmed farther. She glanced at her watch. Joe had been gone for twenty-seven minutes. Was the length of time an indication that he was clearing snow off his helicopter in the hope that he could get it to

run? God, she hoped so, because the other reason he was taking so long was too hideous to contemplate.

Time stretched. She got up and pulled on the coat, the lining felt icy against her already chilled skin. Tugging the long zipper up to her throat, she paced. From the toilet to the vanity and back. Eleven steps. And back again. He'd said he'd be back in an hour. She could wait an hour, even if the flashlight died. She didn't have to go out there and ignore their sympathetic looks, and attempts at making conversation.

Joe please hurry.

How could she possibly feel this deep connection with a man she didn't know? She didn't know the how or the why. She only knew that when this was all over, she wanted to explore what they'd started here.

Shadows formed on the cream and gold wallpaper as she paced back and forth.

Inhale.

Exhale.

The bulb gave up the ghost, plunging the bathroom into stygian darkness. "Well, hell!" Kendall stood in the middle of the bathroom for a couple of seconds waiting for her heart to leave her throat and race

back into her chest. She opened the door. "Hey guys, anyone got a. . ."

Wearing a dark jacket with FBI printed in bright yellow across his chest, Dwight Treadwell leaned against the wall opposite the bathroom door.

He smiled. "Hi, honey. I'm home.

CHAPTER TEN

It could be any one of the men in the house standing there in the semi-darkness. He was little more than a shadowy figure but recognition was instantaneous. Kendall knew who he was almost before she heard the voice.

His voice. Oh, God. The FBI guy hadn't been the FBI guy. He was Treadwell.

Heart pounding, throat dry, Kendall jumped back and tried to slam the bathroom door closed with both hands. It was snatched out of her grasp.

OhGodohGodohGod.

They were close to the same height, in fact now that she saw him again Kendall was stunned at how weedy he looked. In her nightmares he was always huge and brutish. But the reality was Treadwell was medium. Medium height. Medium coloring. Medium features.

His face was ruddy with the cold and excitement. Snot dripped onto his upper lip, and his almost colorless eyes held a mad and terrifyingly familiar gleam. She'd given him that raised red scar running from under his chin to the corner of his lower lip.

His strength was almost superhuman as he grabbed her by the front of her thick coat and yanked her out into the hallway. She fought him wildly, kicking and scratching, screaming bloody murder at the top of her lungs.

He backhanded her, a punishing blow that had her sagging, weak and fighting not to pass out. Not from the pain, but from the memory of all that had come *after* the blows, almost paralyzing her with horror.

"Tsk. Tsk. Now is that any way to welcome an old friend?"

Cheek on fire, legs like rubber, she scrambled to get her feet under her. Shooting out his hand, he fisted the front of the extreme weather coat in one gloved hand and with the other jerked her upright, pulling her into the kitchen by her hair.

The *empty* kitchen.

His fine, light brown hair was wet, as were the shoulders of the too large black ski jacket with the yellow lettering. "Know how many *shit* cars I had to

drive to get to you?" he demanded, shoving her in front of him.

"Know how many *dumb fucks* contributed to the cause, and gave their lives so I could be here with you? Do you, huh? Do you have any idea how *fucking* cold it was hiding out in the trees waiting for just the right moment for us to be reacquainted?"

He shoved her hard and she staggered because he was still holding her hair. Her scalp stung. "Selfish." Shove. "Selfish." Shove. "Bitch."

"Go to hell where you belong." Kendall stumbled before getting her feet under her. Her face throbbed, her scalp burned. Her heart skittered, missed several beats, then raced making her lightheaded. The pantry/safe room was about fifteen feet behind him. If she could get inside, she'd just have to wait until Joe and the others came back.

"You won't get away with this. The place is crawling with cops and the FBI," she whispered through dry lips. Where were they? Dead? He wore an FBI jacket. . .

Her brain was completely blank with terror made worse by the smell.

The familiar, sickening, gut-wrenching smell of fresh blood.

"Not really," Treadwell smiled, using the blade of the knife in his other hand to point at something across the room.

She did not want to look. Bile rose in the back of her throat. It took several eternities for Kendall to force her eyes to shift from the faint glimmer of steel to the dark shape almost lost in the darkness on the floor. "You killed them."

JoeJoeJoe. Acidic bile rose in her throat as she watched him, waiting for an opening to get away. She couldn't think of Joe laying out in the snow, bleeding. Injured. Dead.

"Oops. My bad. Not my best masterpiece." He waved to indicate the blood splattered wall. "Yet. You'll change that." He shoved her away from him. "Go on. Go. Run. Don't make this easy for me, baby."

He slammed his fist into her shoulder when she remained paralyzed. She staggered back a step. His closed fists weren't meaty or large. She'd been mesmerized, in a horrific way, by his hands before. They were narrow and pale, with fingers like a piano player. Or a scalpel-wielding lunatic.

"Go on. Run like the wind, pretty girl. Let old Dwight have a little fun to make up for all the aggravation you caused him."

She was already walking carefully backwards, and his next shoulder slam made her totter. Her hip hit the center island with a dull thud. She fumbled to insert her hand into her coat pocket as she righted herself. It crossed her numb mind for all of a nanosecond that she should keep him talking until she could get her gun from her pocket.

Think! Think! Talk! Treadwell likes to talk, to taunt. If he's talking, he isn't killing me.

Now *It's the Most Wonderful Time Of The Year* was playing. The situation was surreal. God. If he'd killed the cops, and an FBI agent, what about Joe? The image of Joe's body out there in the snow made her sick to her stomach. Kendall swallowed with difficulty as her icy fingers closed around the handle of the LadySmith. She whipped out the .22. The air smelled sweet, unpleasantly so. Nausea rose in her throat at the sickening reek of death.

"There'll be more cops," she told him, arms extended. Keeping her voice steady she clicked off the safety. "They won't stop until they catch you and put you back in your cage."

He smiled, not acknowledging the small gun in her hand. "Maybe. But I'll kill you first, pretty girl. I'll just kill you dead fir—"

Kendall pulled the trigger.

Pop.

The shot made no impact. He didn't fall back or so much flinch, making her doubt she'd hit him at all.

"Bulletproof vest, baby doll. That FBI guy was very accommodating."

"They already have a massive manhunt out looking for you. Your face has been plastered on every TV across the country. You're even more famous now, Dwight. What will they do to you when they find out you killed one of their own? They know *everything* about you, everyone you know and love. There won't be a place you can run, not a place where you can hide. You already have a target on your back. Now they'll smell the blood in the water. You're a dead man."

She backed up inch by inch. Keep him talking. Get inside the safe room.

"Like I give a flying fuck?" he laughed, eyes mad as he jabbed the scalpel in her general direction. "You put me in a fucking *cage* you goddamn bitch."

Everything moved in slow motion as though she were under water, yet images bombarded her. The familiar, sickening glint of the scalpel, the older cop dead at her feet in a dark, slick pool of blood.

The flickering lanterns on the center island cast dancing demonic shadows on Treadwell's face as he kept coming, his expression feral, not slowed in the least by the shot. The knife, small and lethal, slick and already stained with blood.

Pop.

With a howl of pain, he staggered back clutching his ear with his free hand. Blood trickled between his fingers, and his eyes went black with rage. He kept coming. "I'm gonna peel your skin off your body real slow, bitch. Run if you can."

Damn it. She hadn't hit him where it would stop him. God, it barely slowed him down, and he kept coming like a psychotic Frankenstein. Backing away, she felt a total sense of unreality as she fired again. This time she got him in the leg.

Not bad. Except that she'd been aiming for his groin, but he was moving like a drunk, and her aim while not wild, wasn't on target. He yelped in outrage, but other than putting a hitch in his step, the wound didn't stop him.

He flung himself at her, knocking her flat on her back. The gun went skittering across the floor as the back of her head bounced on the unforgiving tile. Kendall saw black snow.

Nononono.

Do not pass out.

You've got this. Don't freak. Breathe.

She'd been trained for this. Trained hard. She was good. Strong. Smart. She knew how to shoot. She'd been taught to protect herself with whatever was at hand. And if there was nothing, she'd improvise.

The scalpel flashed an inch above her nose as he teased her with it. The scar on her throat throbbed.

Treadwell lay half across her body, pushing her hips down with his chest. She used the heel of her hand to slam up into his chin. His teeth snapped as his head jerked back, and he gave a howl of surprise.

Kendall rolled/scurried, crab-like out of the way. Scrambling to regain her footing, she braced a hand on the cabinets of the island, then stomped him in the balls with her entire weight.

His shriek was high and piercing.

While he gagged and clutched his groin, she ran. Around the island, toward the safe room.

Treadwell lunged, grabbing the back of her coat, trying to pull her down. But he did so doubled over with pain, crying and choking. His free hand swung the sharp scalpel in a blind arc.

Grabbing up one of the heavy baking sheets off the counter with both hands, Kendall lifted it high as she swung around, bringing it down with all her strength on his arm. Cookies flew in every direction. Not releasing the scalpel, he fell to one knee screaming obscenities and threats.

She swung again. This time slamming him across the nose with the metal sheet. He howled with rage, lunging blindly, catching her around the back of her knees with both arms in a weird bear hug. Blood streamed from a deep cut above his eye, already swelling shut.

Blood and snot poured from his nose in a bubbly mess. He swiped the back of his hand across his face, eyes murderous as he lunged to his feet.

Kendall slammed the cookie sheet down again. The edge caught his temple and his eyes rolled back. The sheet flew out of her hands to clatter on the tile floor nearby.

Staggering to her feet with more haste than speed, she knew adrenalin alone was blocking any pain she might be feeling. From experience she knew that wouldn't last. She didn't slow down.

A passing glance at the debris-strewn floor indicated no freaking sign of her gun.

So be it. The safe room was filled with guns and just ten feet away.

Treadwell was still gagging and sobbing, half curled over, but he hadn't passed out, and damn if that scalpel wasn't still clutched in the white grip of his bloody fingers. He was between her and the saferoom.

She ran. Around the island, around the bodies of the men blocking the way into the great room, around scattered plastic tubs of Christmas ornaments and garlands. Jumped the hurdle of a box filled with artificial snow. Crunchy, glittering shaved styrofoam spread out to mingle with the congealing pools of blood at her feet.

Knee high boots, meant for strolling in snow, weren't conducive to running. She felt as though she was moving in slow mo. The open doorway seemed to be getting farther away instead of closer. Her foot twisted as she stepped on something hard. Her LadySmith.

With ice cold fingers she scooped it up as she moved, then clutched it tightly and shoved it into her coat pocket. It was all she had, and she was damned if he'd make her drop it again.

Hurryhurryhurry.

Her head jerked back, and her feet lost purchase as Treadwell grabbed her by her hair, slamming his knee

into the small of her back. The impact made bile rise in her throat. He dragged her backwards by the convenient handle she'd made of her upswept hair.

With a scream of blind rage, she wrenched away, feeling the pain as a chunk of her hair was left clutched in his fingers. She ran flat out into the entry hall with a view of the great room's half decorated tree. Joyous Christmas music still played on the portable radio. The room smelled of cinnamon, cookies and blood.

Her feet felt ridiculously clumsy in the heavy snow boots as she bolted for the stairs. Safe room. Master bedroom. *Go go go.*

She only noticed a man's body seconds before she stumbled over him in the entry hall.

Oh, God damn it. It was that sweet kid Sonny, his eyes wide, a gaping hole in his temple where Treadwell had stabbed him.

She jumped at the last fraction of a second, then almost tripped over an askew area rug. Blood made the floor slick, but she skated until she found her balance, lunging for the massive wrought iron handle on the front door. If the door was locked she was screwed. Her fingers tightened around the grip of the small gun.

She screamed as his fingers tangled in her hair, yanking her toward him. She kicked backwards, sending

him into the slippery pool of blood. Losing his footing, he almost took her with him, but Kendall risked a few bald spots by jerking her hair out of his grip again. He went careening into the opposite wall with an inhuman scream of rage.

The heavy door swung open, letting in a blast of frigid air. Without looking back, she darted outside. The icy air stole her breath. The sky had lightened to a dark pewter. The landscape before her looked like a Currier and Ives painting rendered in black and white. An enormous snowplow loomed in the front yard. Were the keys in it? Did she have time to look? How fast did the damn thing go? Fast enough to outrun Treadwell? She couldn't chance taking the time to find out.

She looked around frantically. Where to hide? Where the hell to hide? The son of a bitch was like the Energizer Bunny. He wouldn't stop. Not while he still had a breath in his body.

Chest heaving, she gulped glacial, painful air, hard and fast. Half a mile away were the empty cottages, and/or trees behind which she could hide. She hauled ass across the wide porch knowing he was right behind her.

A flash of silver arced down to her left. She tried to dodge. But his knife ripped through her left sleeve.

No pain. Just an ice-cold jolt as the blade sliced through fabric and down to skin. But it would hurt later. God would it hurt later when adrenaline and fear weren't anesthetizing her.

Run. Run. Run.

He tackled her from behind, taking her down. Her head slammed on the wood floor of the porch, hitting hard, but she tucked and rolled as she'd been taught, managing to stagger back to her feet before he could grab hold of her again. She turned to race down the five steps leaning away from the house.

He grabbed her arm, swinging her into a support column with teeth-jarring impact. Lights, garland and faux candied fruit bounced down the steps. He pulled her up by her collar, then clamped her throat in a one-handed vise.

"Stupid. Stupid, bitch!" his voice, as always, was chillingly calm. Which made it more frightening and ominous than if he'd been yelling at the top of his lungs. "You ruined it. You ruined it *all*."

He smashed the hilt of the knife into her cheekbone. She screamed with the blinding, white hot pain. Brilliant dots danced in her vision as she struggled to stay conscious. It was a losing battle. There was a fuzzy buzz in her ears, then she slipped into silence.

Minutes, hours, *days* later, Kendall came to in a rush of cold, and bone-deep terror.

Oh, God. Oh, God. Treadwell had her slung over his shoulder like a sack of potatoes.

Déjà vu.

They weren't in the front yard. Her hair hung over her face, and she surreptitiously parted the strands. She couldn't see the house. Or the snow plow. Or Joe.

Joe.

Her arm was on fire. The pain intense. Nausea choked her. She heard nothing over the blood pounding in her ears, although the trees must be rustling in the wind, and his boots surely must be making a rhythmic sound as he trudged through the virgin snow.

The wind whipped her hair silently about her head as she hung there like a bat, upside down, almost blinded by the dancing, swirling red strands and the blood rushing to her brain. She forced herself to remain limp. But it wasn't easy. Every fight and flight instinct screamed at her to do something. She wanted to ask him about Joe but didn't dare. She focused on that for a second, reasoning that if Treadwell had killed Joe, he'd have told her as much. She'd learned that about him during her captivity. Treadwell liked to regale her with the gory details of past trophies.

She knew she just had to hang on long enough for Joe to realize that Treadwell had her. Just long enough for him to find her. Please God make it soon. Oh, God. Please. . . Her arm wasn't totally useless. She might not be able to move it, but hot red blood dripped freely from her fingertips onto the pure white snow.

She was leaving a trail of blood in Treadwell's footprints. She could only pray that he didn't look back. That Joe was still alive and able to follow them.

She swallowed convulsively, a blend of bile and terror. She didn't want him to know she was conscious. She could. . . Would- As soon as-

She ruined the element of surprise by puking down his back.

"Jesus! You fucking bitch!" Treadwell growled, flinging her off his shoulder so she landed face first in the snow.

He hauled her to her feet, but she wrenched out of his hold, almost dislocating her shoulder in the process.

Run. Run. Run.

She felt as if she was looking through the bottom of a thick glass. Tree branches slapped at her, though she'd stopped feeling pain hours ago. Clutching her bleeding arm, she ran.

Her life depended on it.

He grabbed her around the neck from behind. She bucked and jerked, leaning her weight to counter his, hoping to slow him down. Keeping her completely off balance, Treadwell dragged her through frozen quicksand toward the tree line. Every time she tried to pull away, he found another place to cut her. Her bright yellow coat was trailing ribbons of fabric. Many of them now tinged red. Kicking and biting. Screaming hoarsely as he took her deeper and deeper into the isolated landscape farther and farther away from the house.

She saw a snowmobile up ahead between the dark skeletons of the trees, black against the brilliance of the snow.

No! Nonononono!

"This has been fun, Kendall." He spun around, grabbing her by the throat, squeezing hard enough for brilliant stars to explode before her eyes. "But you're boring me now. Time to say buh-bye."

Her weight was balanced against his chest and he used his knee as a wedge between her legs, freeing his hand to grab her hair at the scalp as he brought the knife to her throat.

Paralyzed, Kendall stared at the knife inches from her face. "Not again. Damn you, not again."

Despite the pain in her scalp where he'd fisted her long hair, she wrenched her arm up, the small gun clutched in her bloody hand.

Two bullets left.

Make. Them. Count.

She pointed the barrel over her left shoulder and pulled the trigger.

CHAPTER ELEVEN

Joe pushed through the snow, following the blood trail deeper across the vast expanse of snow-covered south paddock toward a small wooded area.

KendallKendallKendall. An insistent mantra in his brain.

Fear was a new experience for him. But it was real and physical. He'd heard her cries on the way back from the disabled chopper. Heard them, and knew immediately that Treadwell had her. And if Treadwell had her, the men he'd assigned to protect her were dead. Ah, Jesus.

Every breath was an effort in the icy air, his heart pounded with helpless frustration at his slow progress in the fresh, calf-deep snow.

Uncharacteristically bloodthirsty images kept flipping through his mind as he ran, weapon drawn in his gloveless hand. He'd learned some interesting techniques with a knife himself over the years. He relished demonstrating his skill to Treadwell. Let the psycho feel the terror of finding *himself* on the other end of a knife wielded by a madman.

A madman who'd been trained in the art of knife fighting, and was fucking used to fighting dirty.

The frigid wind whipped Joe's hair about his face and bat-winged his coat about his body as he ran. Kendall's cries, echoing in the isolation of the remote area, pierced him to the heart.

She was alive. At least he had that to hold onto.

He doubled his effort to reach her as fast as humanly possible as powder skipped and danced across the surface of the drifting snow trying to obliterate Treadwell's footsteps and the obscene splatters of bright blood.

He felt the beat of chopper blades overhead before he heard them. Three coming in fast, spotlights strafing the snow-covered landscape. The cavalry after all. Snow whipped up, blinding him. Damn it to hell- He pointed in the direction of the tree line. Not that they would be able to land here. The terrain was hilly, and there were just too many damn trees. The three beams of light rose, then moved off, taking their lights with them.

Kendall cried out again.

"I'm coming, sweetheart, hold on! I'm coming!" Correcting slightly to the west, he battled across the snow drifts, chest heaving, thighs burning with each high step into the drifts.

He was close. Two hundred yards and closing.

Go. Go. Go.

They were twined as closely as lovers, two indistinguishable silhouettes against the stark whiteness of the snow.

Faster. Faster.

A gunshot cracked through the predawn quiet. Joe's heart jerked in response. *Kendall. . .*

A hundred and fifty- forty- thirty- twenty- He saw the fiery blaze of her hair, the brilliant yellow of her coat, as she and Treadwell fell to the ground in a tangle of arms and legs and started rolling about. Joe saw the glint of a knife in the powerful beam of his Mag light.

Run, faster, damn it, *run*. Ninety feet- eighty- He took aim.

Treadwell and Kendall rolled just as he was about to squeeze off the shot. Shit. She blocked. They rolled again, this time Treadwell on top. Joe fired. The other man jerked with the impact. He tilted.

Sixty feet- forty-

Kendall took the window of opportunity and shoved and pushed Treadwell off of her. God Almighty! Instead of *running*, she surprised the hell out of Joe by jumping on top of Treadwell with a banshee scream of rage. Straddling the man's waist, she started beating the hell out of his head and shoulders with her fists.

Twenty feet- Ten- *Kendall*- Joe grabbed her arm, flinging her aside just as Treadwell's knife arced toward her chest. He grabbed the killer's wrist, placed his weight on the knee he applied to the man's chest, then dug the muzzle of the H&K*hard* to the underside of the guy's chin.

"Play with *me*, dick. " Joe's voice was low and feral as he applied pressure to a tendon in Treadwell's knife hand.

The hold should've caused his fingers to release, but Treadwell's fingers, slick with blood, remained fisted around the hilt of the gleaming surgical knife. Joe dug his knee into the man's chest and exerted more pressure on his wrist.

"Talk to me Kendall," he yelled, keeping his eyes fixed on the killer. "Talk to me, sweetheart!"

"I-I'm okay," she replied, out of his line of sight.

"I won't go back there," Treadwell told Joe vehemently, eyes wild, FBI coat splotched with blood. It

sure as hell better not contain one drop belonging to Kendall. "You can't make me." He attempted to jerk his hand free. "Not going to happen. I won't go back."

Joe kept up the pressure of his thumb on the man's wrist, but the scalpel remained firmly in Treadwell's bloody, but bloodless hand. In one lithe move Joe surged to his feet, dragging Treadwell up with him. The fingers he had around the knife hand remained there like a vice, his weapon stayed put under the weak jaw.

"Oh, you don't have to go back if you don't want to," Joe assured him with silky menace. "In fact, I insist that you d-"

"Oh, God! Joe, watch out!"

He felt the sharp jab of pain in his side a second before Kendall's warning. Damn it to hell! Treadwell producing a second knife – bigger and considerably more effective – and stabbed him right through the hide of his coat. Ah, crap. The other man was also left-handed.

Twisting to deflect the depth of the strike, Joe lifted the H&K. *Pop. Pop.*

Pop.

Treadwell's eyes widened in surprise as he crumpled to his knees, then slowly toppled to his side.

His sightless eyes stared at the dawn flooded sky as bright arterial blood drenched the snow at Joe's feet a satisfying crimson.

Joe plucked both knives from Treadwell's limp fingers. He'd only fired two shots.

Kneeling, he felt for a pulse beneath the crazy bastard's jaw. Dead. Perfect. He turned his head to see Kendall, eyes narrowed, still standing in the classic firing stance.

She looked like an avenging angel with her red hair blowing in the wind, the golden glow of a new day backlighting her. "Is he dead?"

"As the proverbial doornail." Joe assured her as he rose. He kept his gaze on her face as he tossed aside both knives and walked toward her.

"I'm not sure exactly what that is," Kendall said with only a small tremor in her voice. "But if it's very dead I'm all for it."

"Very," Joe assured her, touching the blood on her cheek, and using every ounce of willpower not to fly into a murderous rage and kill Treadwell again.

"But you won't mind if I check for myself?"

"You shot him, I insist."

"I did. Didn't I?" Kendall crouched beside the body, feeling under Treadwell's chin for a pulse.

"Well?" he asked after several moments filled with her ragged breathing and the susurrus of the snow drifts blowing across the surface of the snow between the tree trunks.

With his help, she got to her feet. "Dead as a doornail."

She wrapped her arm around his waist and leaned her head against his chest. Joe wrapped both arms around her. The perky yellow coat was slashed to ribbons, she was shuddering with cold and the sudden loss of adrenaline that had kept her going. Fuck it, it kept her *alive*.

She needed medical attention, and he had to get her out of the frigid wind which was picking up again. "Did he cut you?"

She shook her head against his chest. "No."

"Liar. How bad?"

"Bet I won't need one stitch," she assured him, clutching the front of his coat in both hands as she stood in the circle of his arms. Her casual tone was hard won, the terror was still clear in her expressive eyes.

An unfamiliar aching tenderness gathered inside him. He had to clear the thickness from his throat before he could speak. "You won't mind if I play doctor later, and check that out for myself."

"No *playing*. If you want to be my doctor you have to take the job seriously," Kendall's lips curved. "I insist on a complete and thorough physical."

"I concur. Top to bottom and everything in between. Let's get the hell out of Dodge before then. Come on." He wrapped his arm around her, and they walked between the trees and out into a paddock.

A grudging dawn painted the pristine snow a sullen gray/pink as Joe swung her into his arms.

In the distance he saw the posse arriving. Dozens of local cops, Feebs, and Federal Marshals racing across the tinged snow toward them. There'd be questions and more questions-

He veered off and headed in the opposite direction. "How do you like the great outdoors so far?" he asked conversationally.

She pulled a comical face as she looped her arms around his neck. "Not very."

"Yeah, I can see how the situation would require some rehabilitation," Joe sighed. "The kids would like it out here, though."

She shot him an amused glance as they walked. "Whose?"

"Ours." He rubbed her arm. "Four do you think?"

"Don't you think we should go on a few dates before we start naming our children?"

"How many?"

"Children?"

"No *dates*. How many dates would you consider appropriate?"

"Your call."

"Okay. Three."

They came to the snowmobile Treadwell had left under the trees. "Hop aboard," Joe said, helping her maneuver onto the machine.

"Aren't we a couple of stages beyond dating?" He asked politely, starting the engine.

"No," Kendall told him, wrapping her arms about his waist and resting her cheek on his back. "We are not several stages past dating. I want movies, and dinners, and flowers. You can start by calling me."

The snowmobile picked up speed. Anticipation made Joe's heart pick up speed too. Four miles to a bed. "I don't have your phone number," he shouted as the wind carried them forward.

"I programmed it into your cell phone last night," Kendall laughed, her breath warm against his cheek.

They burst through the trees. Ahead was a pristine expanse of white, pure and fresh and untouched. It held only a few small shadows and was tinged with the promise of sunshine. Kendall tightened her arms about his waist as they approached the house and he shut off the engine.

A group of grim, foot-stamping men waited for them on the porch.

Kendall averted her gaze from two men carrying one of the bodies out of the house to a waiting snowmobile. "I hate to be ungrateful, but how soon can we get rid of them?"

Joe helped her off the snowmobile. "Let's have doc Campbell take a look at you. He's the one in the brown coat. While he checks you out, I'll answer questions and speed them on their way."

The rest of the men were returning from their trek across the snowy field, looking none too happy.

Joe hugged her against his side as her feet faltered in the soft snow. "While doc looks at that arm, I'll hook up the Christmas light's generator to the water heater so you can take a nice hot shower and defrost. Take your time. I've got this.

CHAPTER TWELVE

Treadwell was dead.

The relief Kendall felt was so profound her body shook with the realization that she was really free. Her mind was numb. Emptied of the awful images branded there for so long.

She'd gotten away from him *again*.

Thanks to the courageous man who had, in the process, stolen her heart. Joe had taken charge, fielded all of the questions from the local cops and insisted the taciturn, white-haired doctor attend to her immediately and thoroughly.

The cut on her arm hadn't required stitches after all. The doctor cleaned her abrasions and applied a few butterfly bandages on her cuts. He then prescribed a hot bath for her aches and pains which she gladly agreed to do. Kendall had felt worse, much worse.

It *was* over.

A sob caught in her throat as she closed her eyes and rested her head on the rim of the tub. She would've gotten warmer more quickly if Joe had joined her. She waited for him to burst into the bathroom and join her in the decadently ginormous tub. Part of why she'd stayed neck-deep in the jetted tub until her skin started turning pruney. It was no real hardship.

It had taken a long time to gradually keep adding warmer and warmer water until she had it hot enough to pinken her skin. After she got used to it, the hot water felt amazing against her frozen skin.

As tempting as it was, she couldn't stay in the nice, toasty warm bathroom forever. She'd probably been in there for an hour.

For all she knew, he'd left with the others now the danger to her had passed. But if he'd left, surely he would've come to say goodbye?

She'd put her number in his phone, but she had no idea how to contact *him*. Was T-FLAC listed? She doubted it. And if he'd left without telling her, he probably didn't want her to contact him anyway, despite his words and actions earlier.

It was weird she'd bonded with him in such a short time. Maybe fear had imprinted him onto her. Maybe the fact that he'd been here to protect her had

been the turn on? Maybe it was because he was sexy and intense and there for her when she needed him? Hell, maybe, it was just incredible chemistry that had nothing to do with danger, fear or Treadwell. Whatever the reason, Kendall felt the connection down to her marrow. Yet, another thing to discuss with her therapist.

"And a hell of a lot of good thinking like this is going to do me." There was no reason to stay in Montana. If she could get a flight out tomorrow, she'd surprise her family and spend the holidays in Chicago. They'd be thrilled to see her.

While there was power, she applied eye makeup, and dried her hair before dressing in the long, stretchy red velvet dress she'd planned to wear to the Christmas party. Even if Joe wasn't in the house, Kendall felt more human with makeup on.

She had no idea what plans he'd had to cancel to be here with her.

Would he spend Christmas with friends? A girlfriend?

A look out of the window before she went downstairs showed the sky low and gray. It looked as though it was going to snow again. There were dozens of deep ruts in the pristine snow from the various vehicles coming and going, an indication that the small army of men had left. She winced seeing the giant crack in the tree near the front steps of wrap-around deck, that had nearly scared her to death when it had ripped under the weight of snow. Was that only a few hours ago?

"Joe?" Kendall called hopefully when she hesitated half way down the stairs, afraid of what she'd see. The lights were on, and it was clear there were no bodies, no blood, no sign that anything dramatic had happened here at all. It was surreal seeing the Christmas decorations looking exactly as they had done before she fled the house.

The mouthwatering smell of bacon mingled with that of cinnamon and pine. Her stomach rumbled.

"Kitchen," he called out.

She let out the breath she'd been holding as she got to the bottom of the stairs and turned into the brightly lit kitchen where the savory smells made her mouth water. Bacon. Pancakes. Eggs.

There were no signs of a struggle. No indication of the violence and mayhem that had trashed the kitchen earlier. It was a bit surreal seeing Joe, spatula in hand, look up as she walked into the kitchen as if nothing untoward had happened.

"Everybody left. I answered all the questions to their satisfaction." Putting the spatula down, he came

around the island, his eyes never leaving her face. Extending his hand palm up, he looked her up and down. Slowly. "God, you're gorgeous."

He was gorgeous. The air in her lungs evaporated as Kendall placed her hand in his, palm to palm. His warm fingers closed over hers. His hair was damp and finger combed off his face. Wearing jeans and his cream Aran sweater he looked more delicious than the bacon smelled.

Kendall smiled all the way to her bare toes. "I'm impressed. You showered *and* made breakfast?"

And someone got rid of the blood and gore, thank God. "There's no sign anything happened here. How on earth did they clean up everything so fast? I know it felt as though we were out there forever, but it couldn't have been *that* long."

"T-FLAC cleaners. They do this for a living."

She shuddered. "What a horrible job."

"Unfortunately, they're kept quite busy."

"Let's change the subject." She indicated his jeans, which emphasized his long legs. He too was barefoot. "Did you raid our host's closet?"

The blinds were raised and the light coming in through the large expanse of the kitchen windows was pale, but the spots in the ceiling brightly illuminated the

entire country style kitchen, and did wonderful things to the planes of Joe's strong features. His freshly shaved jaw made Kendall long to cup his face. She resisted.

"I did." He drew her over to the breakfast nook, where he'd removed the stack of plastic tubs filled with decorations, and set the table with a fir-green tablecloth. He'd found the square, white Christmas dishes with stylistic sprays of red berries and green holly leaves and set the table. The centerpiece was one of the small, decorated potted rosemary trees, twinkling with battery operated lights, from an upstairs bedroom.

"Come and sit," he guided her to the end of the banquette seat against the wall. "This is our first date."

"It's a perfect first date." Her heart galloped pleasantly, and a sense of euphoria made anything seem possible. The rush of endorphins made her giddy.

She smiled as she slid onto the long seat. "This looks fabulous. You went all out." It was the sweetest thing a man had ever done for her. She wouldn't have thought, in a million years that a guy like Joe Zorn could ever be called sweet.

He hadn't looked 'sweet' when he'd confronted Treadwell earlier. He hadn't looked sweet at all. He'd looked like a guy who'd kill without a second's thought.

"I hope my culinary attempts impress the hell out of you. I don't do a lot of cooking." He left her at the table and went to open the warming drawer to withdraw several platters which he brought back to the table. "I figured you'd need some downtime. I didn't want to interrupt you. Hope it was long enough for you to regain your equilibrium. Believe me, I should get a prize for my restraint in not coming upstairs to join you in the tub. Coffee, black, right?"

That was a long speech for Joe.

Tummy growling, Kendall adjusted two trivets so he could place the hot dishes on the table. "I'll get it." She started to slide off the cushioned bench seat.

"Stay put." Instead of the fancy coffee machine, he'd made coffee in the same pot she'd used on the stove. He returned with two steaming red mugs.

She took hers in both hands as he slid in on the other side of the table. Instead of staying there, he scooched over to her side of the bench seat, hip to hip. "We need to fast track." His eyes gleamed wickedly as he cast her a sideways glance. "Twenty-one questions?"

The air between them sizzled with awareness. With danger off the table, Kendall felt buoyant and optimistic. And unwilling to let this moment pass. "We could just sort of – you know? Skip to the chase?"

He gave her a stern look. "Absolutely not. You said three dates. You didn't stipulate the time frame, however. I say we have until this afternoon." He dished up crisp bacon, fluffy scrambled eggs, and two, slightly charred pancakes on a separate plate, and added a twig of faux Christmas tree as garnish which made her smile.

"Favorite color?" He passed her the syrup bottle as she plucked the plastic greenery off her eggs.

The heat of his thigh pressed along the length of hers seemed to burn her skin.

Kendall rid herself of the 'garnish', then poured syrup on her pancakes. Starving, she picked up her fork. "Purple. You?" She forked a drippy bite into her mouth. Sweetness exploded on her tongue.

"Marmalade." He ran his palm over her hair, then leaned in to lick a little drop of maple syrup off the corner of her mouth with a flick of his tongue.

His dilated pupils were ringed with a sliver of intense blue as he lifted his head.

The clean, soapy smell of his skin went to her head making her dizzy with longing. Damn it, she craved more than a quick kiss. Turning, she tapped her lower lip. "You missed some."

"Three dates. . ."

"*Whatever*. Kiss me!"

Her breath snagged in her throat as his head lowered, blocking out the light. With a small sigh, Kendall closed her eyes, parting her lips to welcome him. He stroked her face with gentle fingers, tipping up her jaw to better angle her mouth. She breathed him in, wanting him with a strength and desperation that should have frightened her. Instead her belly quivered with anticipation, and moisture dewed between her legs.

She opened her eyes.

The tight intensity of his expression should've scare her to death. Instead Kendall curled her fingers into the springy wool of his sweater, feeling the rock-hard planes of his chest flex under her exploration. She wanted to feel his skin, and dragged her hand down so she could slip her palm under his sweater.

His skin was hot, smooth satin, his abs contracting at her touch.

Bringing his mouth to hers he groaned his pleasure as their tongues rolled and stroked in a mind-bending tangle that had her almost climbing his body to get closer. Impossible to do sitting side by side, although Kendall was practically riding his thigh in an attempt to climb inside him.

Hands tangled in her hair, he nibbled and teased, catching lightly at her lower lip with his teeth,

then played over the little sting with a hot sweep of his tongue. Her breath hitched, but his lips drifted away to stroke a burning path across her cheek, paused over her closed lids, then returned to her eagerly waiting mouth.

She welcomed his tongue, silky-smooth and wet, against hers as he tasted her, the subtle strokes and forays made more thrilling by his control. He didn't plunder. He didn't grab. Instead he savored, which made her feel cherished. It also made her temperature spike and her pulse race with anticipation.

Nor was he immune himself, she felt the fine tremor riding through his body as Joe kissed her. He buried both hands in her hair, cupping the back of her head in one palm as he gently teased her mouth.

Twisting to gain better access, she reciprocated by combing her fingers through the cool, silky strands of his dark hair. She scored her nails gently against his scalp, causing him to draw in an out of rhythm breath, but he didn't stop what he was doing.

When their lips finally parted, she struggled to draw in an even breath. Joe touched her forehead with his. They were both breathing as if they'd run a marathon.

Holding her gaze, he ran the back of his fingers under the edge of the scooped neckline of the velvet

dress, just brushing the upper swell of her breasts but missing the aching peaks of her nipples. She felt that ghost of a touch directly to her core.

"Are you wearing anything under this mind-blowing dress?"

She was not. Her nipples peaked, painfully hard, exquisitely sensitive. "Some things are worth discovering for oneself."

Joe closed his eyes as if in pain and withdrew his hand to pick up his fork in his left hand. His arm brushed hers so that she felt the flex of his muscles as he moved. A shiver of anticipation heated her blood. She licked her bottom lip, tasting the ghost of syrup and wishing she was tasting Joe again instead.

His pupils dilated as he followed the movement of her tongue. She licked her lip again. Slowly.

Joe groaned softly. "Do you go to third base on a first date?"

Kendall's laugh was strained. She leaned into him, pressing her breast against his bicep. The friction caused her nipples to tighten even more. "I never have before. But with the right incentive— "

"*Three* dates," he told her thickly. A diabolical gleam lit his hungry eyes. "Just so you know. I excelled at SERE training."

Vaguely she knew what that was, but teased, "So you grill a mean steak?"

"Survival Evasion Resistance and Escape. Part of my training is to resist enemy interrogation and their torture techniques."

"You think I'm torturing you?" she scoffed settling back on the seat. "Please. I haven't even started."

He groaned. "Then you'd better eat that protein and gather your strength. We have two and a half more dates to go."

Kendall shook her head, the magnitude of how deeply she felt for this man she barely knew, stunned her. "You think you're going to last through two and a half dates?" She cut into her pancake with her fork. "Silly man."

"Happiest memory from your childhood?" he asked, a muscle clenching in his jaw.

Freaking hard to think of a memory when her body was on red alert at the feel of his slick tongue. Despite her hunger for the food in front of her, Kendall wanted Joe more. Switching hands so that she too ate with her left hand, she spread her fingers on his leg, just above his knee. Even through his jeans, his thigh felt like hot steel as it flexed beneath her touch. She slid her palm a little higher.

He gripped her hand. She didn't move it, just waited until he picked up his fork again, and once liberated, slid her palm a little higher.

"I had a great childhood. All my memories are good," she said softly, watching the color of control darken his cheeks as she brushed the tent of his erection. He sucked in a sharp breath as she explored the shape of him through his pants. She'd never been so bold, and she felt the high of stepping outside herself and doing something because it felt right.

"I was incredibly lucky." Taking her sweet time, she glided her palm back down to his knee. "But one of my favorites was my Mom's face the first time I knitted a sweater for her, I was about twelve. Her approval meant- *means*- everything to me. She's always been my champion, my biggest supporter, my rock. I'm grateful for her every day. I hated that they were at the trial, and so damned grateful to have them there supporting me when what they heard was so shocking."

"You weren't responsible."

"Intellectually I know that," her fingers climbed up his thigh again, lingered, circled. "But my heart hurt watching her there, day after day."

"And no doubt she felt the same watching you. Favorite—"

With a shake of her head, Kendall put a finger to his lips. "My turn." His tongue darted out to taste her skin. "H-happiest memory when you were a kid?"

"Eleven years old." His voice was strained as she inched her fingers back to his gratifying hard erection with one hand, and gripped the edge of the table with her other.

The only way she could closer would be to straddle his lap. Kendall was ready to flip the table, dishes and all, and do just that.

"My dad took me camping to Lewis and Clarke State Park. Little log cabin in the woods. I went under duress and ended up loving it."

"I can't imagine you as a little kid." He seemed invincible to her. Under her exploring fingers his penis lengthened and hardened. Moisture pooled between her legs.

"Everyone starts as one," His lips twitched, and he shifted his hips as her fingers circled his length over his jeans. "I'm sure you were the cutest kid in the neighborhood."

"Shy. Painfully so. . . Your SERE training is impressive."

"Top. Of. My. Class." Eyes glazed. he made no pretense of eating. "Favorite drink?"

"Coffee, strong and black." There was no way she could unzip his jeans. He'd have to stand for that. Or lie down. "You?"

He blinked, distracted as he kneaded her breast, his strong fingers gentle as he pinched her nipple. A hot flood of moisture readied her body for sex. Hard, driving, powerful sex. She needed more. More kisses, more touching. She needed him deep inside her. *Now*, damn it.

"Strong and hot." Skin stretched taut across hos cheek bones, he rubbed his thumb back and forth across her nipple. " Favorite thing to eat?"

He was fueling the fire so hot inside her that she was about to explode. She was ready to slide from the bench seat and seduce him. On the floor if necessary. Kendall withdrew her hand from and picked up a slice of crunchy bacon. "Bacon of course. What about y—"

Joe guided her hand to his mouth and took her last piece of bacon between his strong white teeth.

"Hey!"

His smile was wicked as he slid his palm up *her* thigh, bunching the thin velvet fabric to bare her leg. "Trying to hurry things along, I'm hanging by a thread here, Miss Metcalf."

She wanted to taste his smile again. His touch, so close to where she craved it, made Kendall forgot about the barely eaten food on her plate, and that bite of bacon she'd saved for last.

"No need." She slid out of the booth seat, legs weak. "I think we've had enough foreplay, don't you?"

"God yes," Swinging her up in his arms, he touched his forehead to hers and whispered harshly. "Mercy. You broke me. I cave. I give up. I'll tell you all my secrets."

"I should be doing the SERE training. I'm *that* good."

Energy vibrated off him like a tuning fork. Kendall wrapped her legs around his waist as he carried her to the center island, with his hands cupping her butt cheeks to support her. She helped by winding her arms around his neck and tightening her legs around his waist.

"Yes," he said with feeling. "Yes, you are."

Feeling euphoric, she laughed as he set her bare butt on the cold quartz countertop, her spread legs bracketing his hips. Combing her fingers through his hair, she lowered his head, bringing his mouth down to hers. She met the thrust of his tongue thrust for thrust as his fingers closed around her breast. She leaned into him, flattening the pillows of her breasts against his chest, breathing in the smell of him. Soap and musk. A heady combination.

Digging her fingers into his chest, she disengaged their lips to explore. Drunk on lust she stroked her tongue down the pulsing cord on his neck, then dragged her teeth over his skin. The sexual tension between them pulled inexorably tighter until the very air around them seemed to vibrate. She shifted impatiently as every cell in her body gravitated toward him.

He stuck his fingers into his front pocket and pulled out a small foil square.

She almost groaned out loud with impatience. "You carry condoms around with you?" Not that she wasn't eternally grateful, but the fact that he was such a Boy Scout gave her pause. Was he always ready for a quick lay? Worse yet – when had she become a quick lay?

"Let me put it this way," he said, twisting the small package between his fingers. "Con*dom*. There's no plural about it." He trailed the foil up and over her breast making her nipple ache for a firmer, more personal, touch. "And this damn thing is so old I'm not going to guarantee it's reliability. Still game?"

Since he asked the question with his lips against her throat, and his hand sliding purposefully up her inner thigh, Kendall only managed to push out the words

"Then there doesn't seem to be much point using it, considering you only have one, and we have two dates to go."

He tossed the foil pouch over his shoulder. "Done." He brushed his lips around the curve of her ear, causing every nerve in her skin come alive, and nudged her knees apart. "Is that an all systems go?"

She wanted to say something clever and witty, but she barely had enough breath to demand, "I want you inside me. *Now*." And just in case her urgency wasn't coming through loud and clear, she slid her hand down his hip, then wrapped her fingers around his jean encased penis.

She wanted him in her. Around her. Over her. Under her.

"It's broad daylight, the blinds are open and anyone can see in," she felt compelled to remind him. Honestly, she didn't give a damn if someone sold tickets or pulled up a chair. Her body craved release. Now.

"There's no one out there, and even if there was, I don't give a damn." He nudged her arms. "Up."

Kendall raised both arms so he could pull her dress over her head. It would've been faster if she'd ripped it off herself. He took his sweet, sweet freaking time.

CHAPTER THIRTEEN

As still as a statue, she stared up at him, eyes blazing, face flushed as Joe slid the dress up her naked body, inch by inch. He tortured himself by making the reveal painstakingly slow. He didn't think it was possible to get harder or hotter. The soft, stretchy velvet clung to the jut of her nipples until he tugged it free. He tossed her dress aside as he looked his fill.

The heady scent of pears increased with her body heat. The head to toe tension in his body was almost unbearable, and he had to swallow a groan of desperation. He wasn't a fucking saint, but this, *she,* was more important than a quick fuck.

Stroking his hands from her waist to her hips and back again, he murmured, "You take my breath away. If I'd known you were bare-assed naked under that sexy dress, you wouldn't have had a chance to eat one bite of breakfast."

She was so lovely she made his throat ache. His belly cramped with fury seeing the dozens of scars covering almost every inch of her pale body from her throat to her toes. And the butterfly bandages on her upper arm.

It was inconceivable that she'd managed to survive Treadwell. Twice.

She'd shot the fucker dead.

She was a warrior.

A survivor.

The least he could do was pace his impatient self.

As enthusiastic as she seemed, he didn't want to risk freaking her out by doing what he desperately wanted to do. Which was to pound into her until neither of them could see straight. Nothing that smacked of violence, no matter how fucking hot he was for her. No matter how willing she appeared to be. She'd been traumatized enough already.

How long had it been for her? Hell, he didn't even know if she was in a relationship back in Seattle. And if she was? Would the answer make any difference to how much he wanted her? "Boyfriend? Lover? Christ. A *husband* back in Seattle?"

"No. No and no. I haven't been touched since. . . before. Actually,quite a long time before." She brushed his mouth with two fingers.

Joe felt that touch as if an electrical current ran directly from his lips to his dick. He stroked both hands from her shoulders to her wrists.

Delicate, fine-boned.

Scarred.

He closed his eyes. Opened them. "I'm going slowly here, sweetheart. I don't want to spook you with how badly I want to be inside you."

Her breathing was ragged, the pulse at the base of her throat throbbed in time with the throbbing in his tightly confined dick. "Don't be slow. I want you hard and fast."

While he was looking his fill,too afraid to move because his dick was being strangled by his pants. One wrong move would be the end of this encounter.

Her cheeks flushed. Eyes all pupil, she tried to cover herself with her hands, clearly thinking he'd stopped when he got a good look at all the scars. "Sorry. In the dark would be better."

"Never," he tilted up her face with a finger under her chin. "Don't hide from me," his voice was soft, thick with desire. "Every inch of your body makes me hot.

There's not a part of you that I don't want to touch. Taste. Linger over."

Gently he moved her hands so her palms flattened on the counter beside her hips. "Don't ever apologize. Every mark is a badge of courage," Joe's voice was rough with emotion. "And don't ever suggest I look at you in anything other than the brightest of lights. Everything about you turns me on."

The full, pale globes of her breasts were traced with thin blue veins. The pink tips hardened in response to his gaze. Joe gathered her hair into a bunch, then bent his head to inhale her unique fragrance.

Kendall traced a jagged scar that ran across his ribs. "You've been to battle."

"It's what I do."

"Rescue strange women from deranged serial killers?"

He smiled as he cupped her cheek, stroking her soft skin with his thumb. "You're not *that* strange."

"Ha."

Lowering his head, he took a tight bud into his mouth, using a flattened hand on her lower back to draw her more tightly against him. She drew in a breath at the moist suction. Head thrown back, she arched against his mouth with a broken murmur.

Cupping her breast, he stroked his thumb over the hard bud, nibbling his way up her throat, swamped with the heady fragrance of ripe, juicy pears and aroused woman. "I have a major problem," he said hoarsely, licking a path to her ear.

She froze "Oh, God. What?"

"I'm still fully dressed and you're gloriously naked."

She started tugging his sweater up his chest. "I can solve that problem." As soon as it cleared his head, she lay her lips on his and kissed him sweetly, then held his head in both hands and kissed him with tongue until they broke apart breathing heavily.

"Will we survive dating?" she asked, resting her forehead on his, her breathing rough, her skin dewy.

"It's a necessary step to our future." It was the first time Joe had ever considered he *had* a future. He kissed her shoulder and she tilted her head to give him better access.

Kendall gave a half laugh, lifting her head. Her eyes were all pupil, her lips pink and swollen from kissing. "Do I need to cut you out of those jeans?" Her breathing was uneven, her chest rising and falling which distracted the hell out of him. It felt incredible having her slide her hands up his chest. "God, you feel good."

"To ensure the future of our children, it's best if I step away for a moment and get them off myself."

She looked at her bare wrist. "Two seconds. Go."

Joe shoved his pants down, not off.

He couldn't wait that long.

With his arms around her, his dick became a divining rod, plunging into her wet heat without preamble. With a gasp, she clung more tightly to his shoulders, tightening her ankles at the small of his back.

The moment he was deep inside her, they climaxed simultaneously.

Dropping her head to his chest her body clamped around his as her internal muscles spasmed around him. For an eternity, neither could move as the orgasm pulsed and shimmied through their bodies.

Eventually Joe reluctantly unglued their upper torsos. "Well," he said softly, moving a damp strand of coppery hair from her sweaty cheek, "How do you like our first date?"

"More than eager to get to our *second* date," she told him, slipping off the counter to stand in front of him, her magnificent breasts pressed flat against his chest as she slid her arms around his waist. "There were things I missed due to our. . .haste."

"Yeah. I missed a few vital stops along the way. I'm afraid speed might be an issue for several more dates since I can't seem to keep any of my body parts off your body parts because my body parts are overeager. I want you so badly my training is absolutely useless. Thank God you're not a terrorist. I'd be toast."

#

A quick stop in the hall bathroom to clean up and Kendall padded into the great room. She'd grabbed her dress off the floor and now wore it over her over-stimulated body.

"I'm ready for our second date," she told him.

Long red tapers and twinkly white lights from the bottom half of the partially decorated tree lit the room along with the fire leaping in the massive stone fireplace. The drapes were firmly closed, blocking out the thin morning light.

"Movie night accompanied by popcorn. Followed by a lengthy- or as lengthy as we can make it- necking session."

"It's barely nine in the morning, hardly night," she pointed out, bending to pick up a bowl of popcorn so she had something to do with her hands. While she'd redressed, Joe stood there naked, bathed in amber firelight, gloriously erect. His body was big and broad,

his muscles sleek and cut, with not an ounce of fat on him. He looked like exactly what he was. A warrior.

This playful side of him was charming and completely unexpected. And utterly frustrating. "And at the rate we're going we might not be capable of 'lengthy'."

The movie, sound off, was already playing on the large TV. A quick glance showed it was a romance with pretty adults, happy children, licking puppies and Christmas trees. It didn't matter, she had no intention of watching it. "Aren't we a little beyond a necking session?" she asked, about to plop down on her knees on the nest of blankets he'd made in front of the fire.

Joe stopped her with a hand on her upper arm, which he immediately dropped.

With a puzzled frown at his strange behavior, she ate a nub of popcorn and pulled a face. "This popcorn is cold, you know."

"It was popped over an hour ago. Don't eat it, it's merely symbolic." He removed the bowl from her hand.

"Of what?"

"Second date?" He dropped the bowl onto the sofa without looking. "Good Lord, woman, please try to keep up, I'm hanging by a thread here."

Kendall folded her arms, and laughed. "You could just cut to the chase. Clearly I'm more than willing."

"Three dates. *Today*. Then trust me, sweetheart, I'll cut to the chase so long and hard you'll have to stay in bed for a week. Look around. Like what you see for date two?"

The fire. The candlelight. Joe. Naked. "Of course. It's lovel— "

"You said three dates. You'll *have* three dates. If it kills me."

"What if it kills *me*?" Ignore his impressive erection inches from where she wanted it? No way. She reached out to touch.

Eyes glittering, he stepped back. "If you thought date one was too quick, don't touch me now. Date two will be over before it starts." He waved an expansive hand. "Take it all in. We need to progress to date three immediately."

"Fine. What and where is date three? Because. I'm. Freaking *ready*. Right. Now."

"Upstairs. A horizontal surface and a bottle of wine."

"You're on. Race you upstairs." Kendall wasn't sure she could actually run – upstairs no less- when she

was this aroused. Picking up the hem of her dress so she didn't fall flat on her face, she spun on her heel and made a mad dash for the stairs. "If you're not there when I get there," she shouted over her shoulder, "I'm starting without you!"

Joe raced passed her, taking the stairs two at a time.

CHAPTER FOURTEEN

She was easy to catch. She wasn't running very fast.

"You always have on too many damned clothes." He caught her by the waist on the fifth step. Turning she wrapped her arms around his neck as he took her down.

Her mouth curved, and her pretty eyes glittered up at him as she lay, back arched on the stairs as he pulled the dress over her head. "Just stay naked for the duration to save me time, would you?"

She laughed. "You know this is physically impossible, don't y—"

His mouth silenced her. Nothing was impossible.

He braced his hands on the riser on either side of her head as her knees came up to hug his hips. Her hips lifted to greet his first thrust.

It was over in minutes, leaving them with ragged breath and sweat dampened skin.

He sucked in deep, gulping breathes, somehow managing to position himself so that while he was still inside her, he wasn't pressing her against the hard wood of the steps.

"Okay?" he asked, opening his eyes a crack.

Pushing hair off his sweat-damp forehead, she grinned. "Better than. But I think I have bruises on my butt." She screamed playfully as he turned her over to lavish kisses on said butt.

Cradling her cheek on her folded hands Kendall let herself drift. She was limp as a noodle with a mixture of pleasure and exhaustion. Not that she'd noticed while they were in the throws- but now that she wasn't otherwise occupied, she felt each individual plank of wood. Across her upper chest, midriff, hips, thighs and shin bones, just as she'd felt them all the way down her back earlier.

She found just enough energy to turn over, then climbed over his long, rangy body. Let him take the brunt of hardwood for a while. He shifted beneath her, getting comfortable, as he talked. Kendall whiled away the time by kissing his throat, his jaw, his mouth and wherever else she could reach without expending any more energy than necessary.

Joe had shifted them to a prone position, her head supported by his hand, his body sprawled half over hers. His body burned with a furnace heat. His arms were like steel bands surrounding her. Not a cage, but a haven.

He rubbed his slightly stubbled jaw across her lower belly. There were scars there too. Thin white lines that she knew he could see in the dancing firelight.

His skin gleamed and she couldn't resist sinking her fingers into the crisp dark hair that V'd from his chest down to a narrow arrow pointing to his erect penis.

The lights from the room below him limned the dark silhouette of his naked body in bronze as he stretched out beside her. It was a spectacular show.

He was hot, silky and hard. She stroked her thumb over the head until he groaned.

"I plan on exploring every glorious inch of you, Miss Metcalf, but that pleasure will have to—" he groaned as her fingers tightened around him, "wait."

Like the rest of him, Joe was a big guy. He had big- hands. He slid two fingers inside her, circling, massaging and unnecessarily testing her readiness. She'd been wet for the past hour or more. Kendall shuddered, rolling her hips against his hand in jerky,

involuntary motion. She was wet, swollen and desperate. Several stages beyond ‘ready’. "Talk about *chatty.*"

With a huff of laughter, Joe withdrew his hand to settle his hips between her spread knees. She had a moment's pause to feel the sheer size of him – there-before he pushed inside.

He hissed out a shuddering breath as he buried himself to the hilt in one powerful thrust, then lay still. And Kendall was grateful. The sensation of Joe inside her was so piercingly sweet, so monumental, that she couldn’t move either. This time she wanted this to last.

"Okay?" he asked, voice rough against her ear. His skin felt like a furnace the entire length of her body.

She smiled against his throat. "Better than."

"Wrap your legs around me."

"I was getting there." She groused, her voice thick as he pushed himself impossibly deeper. She walked her heels up his back, feeling gloriously invaded, and kissed his jaw as he started to move.

Pinned down by his not inconsiderable weight, her legs tightened as he moved his big, powerful body inside hers. She felt alive, supernaturally so, as she arched and burned and shuddered in his arms.

Their love making transcended anything Kendall could ever have imagined even in her wildest dreams. Their bodies were perfectly matched. Yin and Yang. The waves of pleasure crashed and churned until she went blind and deaf, her entire being focused on where they were joined, as she was helplessly urged higher and higher, impossibly higher, on a tidal wave of sensation.

Breathless and sweaty, they rested, their bodies glued together, their harsh breathing in sync.

After several minutes or hours, Joe scooped her up and carried her upstairs.

"Very manly," she murmured, looping her arms about his neck and laying her head on his chest as he carried her to her bedroom down the hall.

He lay her on the bed, then followed her down, scooping her up and over so she lay on his chest like a curvy blanket. "We've fast-tracked from speed dating, to going steady, to will you marry me, to I think we just made a baby."

Her pretty eyes widened. "*Did* you propose?"

"It appears so."

Kendall bit her lower lip. "We've barely known each other twelve hours, Joe."

"I know all I need to know. We have the next sixty-two years to fill in the gaps. I've never wanted anything or anyone the way I want you. Say yes."

She didn't hesitate. "Yes. Yes. Yes. This is going to be a hell of a story to tell our grandchildren."

The End

A Killer Christmas Personal Guide

(Includes Spoiler's)

Main Characters: Joe Zorn and Kendall Metcalf

Setting: Helena, Montana

Time of Year: Winter

Serial Killer: Dwight Gus Treadwell

Dossier Joe Zorn

Age: Early 30's

Height: A good 5 inches taller than Kendall Metcalf

Hair: Thick, Dark, Silky

Eyes: Steady, Long dark lashes, Cool blue eyes, Steely dangerous.

Body: Pale scar beside his lower lip almost buried in the crease of his smile, Potent smile, Sexy mouth, Lean cheeks, Could use a shave , Craggy, unseasonably tanned face, Massive shoulders, Arms like steel bands, Broad tanned chest, Long legs, Well-endowed in the "male" department, Rugged, Impressive physique bands of taut muscles, A bear of a man, Marlboro man type, Good looking, Sexy looking, Woodsy cologne.

Dress: Thick off-white turtleneck and jeans.

Voice: Deep, Low, Husky, Soothing

Marital Status: Divorced from Denise Cameron

Children: None

Employment: Bodyguard

Education: University of Montana

Skills: Is a pilot, Trained in the art of knife fighting.

Personality & Attitude: Intimidating, Over achiever, Annoyingly bossy, Sex appeal in spades, Has a nomadic lifestyle, A man of action and few words.

Likes & Dislikes: Hates to lose at anything, Loves a mellow brandy on a cold winters night.

Weapons: HK Mark 23 Heckler & Koch double action pistol, Nasty looking black gun he carries in his waistband at the small of his back. Ka-Bar knife.

Background: Played football at the University of Montana, Had been in the Marines with Adam Cameron years ago , His boss is a woman named Roz, Hadn't had a vacation in 2 years, His cell phone plays/rings an old fashioned sound ring tone, Had a "hurry, the justice of the peace is waiting" wedding to Denise Cameron Marriage to Denise only lasted 5 months, Divorced Denise 10 years ago.

Kendall Metcalf

Height: 5'9"

Hair: Red. Distinctive red/gold. Spills over her shoulders like liquid fire, Deep, rich orange-red of an excellent XO Cognac.

Eyes: Large. Sparkling. Hazel.

Body: An Amazon. Attractive. Pale, velvety skin with amber freckles. Nails painted Christmas red. Endearingly too large feet. Luscious. Curvy. Smells of pears. Ugly scar on her throat. Dozens more obscene scars, thin and silvery (defense wounds), all over her.

Dress: Subtle make up. Red sweater and black leggings.

Voice: Robust laugh

Marital Status: Divorced

Children: None

Employment: A designer. A party planner. Owns her own very successful business. Her business partner is Rebecca Metzner.

Personality & Attitude: Smart. Deliberate. Not much of a follower. Likes to think things through. Not that spontaneous of a person. Weighs the pros and cons before making decisions. Funny. Intelligent. Sex appeal off the charts.

Quirks & Habits: Paces. Usually sleeps naked. Bites her lip as she ponders. Babbles when she is nervous. Makes busy work when scared. Scar on her throat

always throbs when she thinks about the night of the attack.

Weapons: LadySmith handgun

Background: Was kidnapped and assaulted 15 months ago by Dwight Treadwell. Tortured for 17 hours by Treadwell. She is his only living victim . Learned that if she kept her body and mind busy enough, she could keep horrific memories at bay. Went to therapy for several months after her attack. Took self-defense classes. Bought a gun and learned to use it. Felt invincible before the Treadwell attack. Had two fairly long term relationships over the last 10 years. Dated Andy for more than 6 months before sleeping with him. Dated Jerry for a year. Cell phone plays/rings Beethoven's Fifth.

Supporting Characters

Adam Cameron: Ex-Marine, Married to Denise Cameron, three children and another on the way.

Denise Cameron: Ex-husband is Joe Zorn, Married to Adam Cameron, doesn't shop at discount stores, no expense spared wedding to Adam, three children and another on the way, married three months after her divorce from Joe, had a "hurry, the justice of the peace is waiting" wedding with Joe Zorn.

Andy: Had dated Kendall for over 6 months before she would sleep with him.

Donald Sanders: Married to Donna Sanders

Donna Sanders: Close to 60, Married to Donald Sanders

Jerry: Had dated Kendall for a year.

McKenna: Montana cop. DECEASED

Preston: From New York

Rebecca Metzner: Aka Becky and/or Beck Kendall's business partner

Roz: Joe's boss

Sonny Goodwin: A cop, A younger brother of one of Joe's old college buddies. DECEASED

William "Buckeye" Wilder: Beefy, Red faced Chief of police, Wore a Stetson, His son had played football with Joe at the University of Montana. DECEASED

The Christophs: Had a nice secluded little summer place over the ridge.

Dwight Gus Treadwell: Fine hair, Light brown hair, Not a big man, Soft fleshy face, Pale narrow hands, Weedy

looking, Medium height, Medium coloring, Medium features, Fingers like a piano player, Chillingly calm voice, Right and left handed, Crazy Serial killer, Determined, Didn't look like a monster, looked like a teacher or a priest. Had kidnapped and abused Kendall, Sharp knives and a ka-bar were his weapons of choice, Knew how to inflict the most exquisitely painful kind of torture , Killed 23 before his arraignment and at least 7 more after his escape, Received 23 consecutive life sentences and one concurrent for attempted 1st degree on Kendall and another 75 years for her torture, Almost superhuman strength.

DECEASED - shot and killed by Kendall and Joe

T-FLAC Background

Terrorist Force Logistic Assault Command

Vitute et Armis Fide Mea Semper Frater

By courage and by arms. On my word of honor.
Always brothers.

As the Cold War fell to bits of rubble, top level government officials and those in the private sector saw a new breed of organization gain momentum. The major threats no longer hinged on the posturing of super powers. An even more dangerous enemy emerged - small, well funded guerilla groups began to drive fear into the lives of people all over the world. They were rich, connected, quiet, determined and often preferred killing to make their point.

Governments paralyzed by the rule of law and international treaties and conventions required months to react. Because of this, a new industry was born - private anti-terrorist organizations. Premier among them is T-FLAC.

Geoffrey Wright, Lucas Sullivan, and Katrina DeGlaure founded T-FLAC utilizing their connections - political, military and scientific. Headquartered at a sprawling complex in Montana, they recruited and trained the first operatives in the 1980s. T-FLAC specialized in difficult, sticky situations, often hired quietly by officials whose hands were otherwise tied.

Every candidate faced a grueling test of ability, courage, ethics and loyalty. For the safety and integrity of the organization field operatives work in small

teams. The identities of operatives is closely held information, shared only on a need-to-know basis. Operatives often go years, even their entire careers - without knowing the identities of the other T-FLAC agents in the organization.

T-FLAC agents know their code by rote. Vitute et armis, Fide mea. Semper Frater. Courage and by arms. On my word of honor. Always brothers.

Agents can be male or female. Young or old. They are your neighbors. Your friends. Your guardians. Protecting the innocent is a calling. Destroying terror wherever it breeds is a mandate.

They are the men and women of T-FLAC.

T-FLAC Mission Statement

Vision: To be the world's leading provider of strategic, logistical and technological solutions while retaining anonymity as individuals.

Mission: Terrorist Force Logistical Assault Command (T-FLAC) effectively and efficiently integrates resources, technology and experience to provide top-level solutions to the most difficult situations. We exceed expectations where others fail. Guided by courage, ingenuity, innovation and a desire for a safer world, T-FLAC professionals utilize state-of-the-art training, innovative technology and logistical solutions to deliver results world-wide. T-FLAC recognizes that in this post-Cold War era, terrorism is the primary threat to democratic principles across the world. Our combat missions are directed at the base of global terror operations. T-FLAC's mission is to eliminate all such threats by all, and any means at our disposal.

T-FLAC Core Values Ethics: For the ancient Greeks, the word meant "character." For Aristotle, the study of ethics was the study of excellence or the virtues of character. It has come to mean the study and practice of the "good life," the kind of life people ought to live.

In our time, the concept of ethics has broadened to include not only the characteristics of the good person, but also the "best practices" in various professions, among them medicine, the law, the military. We are committed to serving, and expect the highest standards of ethical and professional behavior and adherence to a universally accepted core of values from all our employees

Teamwork: There is no "I" in team, just as there is no "I" in T-FLAC. We function as a uniformly coordinated collection of experience and expertise, where all members of the company work to bring about innovation and solutions that serve our mission to the highest degree possible.

Courage: Fear is only that which we have not overcome. In T-FLAC courage is not the absence of fear, but rather the determination that our mission is of more importance than the fear and the resulting strength and focus, which arises from that determination.

Respect: Each member of the team is essential. We give, and expect in return, respect for others, their beliefs, and their unique perspectives and ideas. We realize that like technologically advanced piece of equipment, each element must work with precision, independently, but in unison, to produce precise results.

Innovation: We encourage, appreciate, and seek out the best of the best superior performance in all areas of operations. We recognize that there are always opportunities for improvement and we strive to elevate expectations and exceed in situations that others deem impossible.

Counterterrorism Policy:1. NO negotiation, make no concessions to terrorists.2. Bring terrorists to justice for their crimes no matter who or where they are.3. Isolate and apply pressure on states that sponsor terrorism, forcing them to change their behavior either overtly or covertly.4. Bolster the counterterrorism capabilities of those countries friendly to the mandates of the U.S.5.

Improve counterterrorism cooperation with foreign governments and participate in the development, coordination, and implementation of American counterterrorism policy in accordance with the policies of the United States Government.

International Terrorism:

Hostages:

T-FLAC will make no concessions to individuals or groups holding official or private U.S. citizens hostage. Our operatives will use every resource necessary to gain the safe return of American citizens being held hostage. At the same time, it is our policy to deny hostage takers the benefits of ransom, prisoner releases, policy changes, or other acts of concession.

Areas of Expertise:

- Find and retrieve critical personnel and/or property
- Full-range of armaments
- Hard target and soft target risk assessment
- Critical infrastructure assurance
- Physical elimination of terrorist cells
- Homeland and executive security
- Combat/demilitarization
- Nonproliferation/counter-proliferation
- Intelligence
- Private protection of Foreign Dignitaries

- Counterintelligence
- Persons of Special Interest - Snatch and Grab

T-FLAC Covert Operatives

AJ COOPER: Operative - Out of Sight, Hot Ice

ALEX STONE: Operative (PSI Unit) - Edge of Danger, Edge of Darkness

ALEXANDER "LYNX" STONE: Operative - The Mercenary, Hide & Seek

APOLLO HAWKINS: Operative (In Cairo) - Out Of Sight

ARITARIQ: Operative (In Cairo) Out Of Sight

ASH: Operative - On Thin Ice

ASHER DAKLIN: Operative - Hot Ice

AUSTIN: Operative - Hot Ice

BANTHER: (Deceased) Operative - White Heat

BURTON: Operative - Hot Ice

CALEB EDGE: Operative (PSI Unit) - Edge of Danger, Edge of Darkness

CAROL: Nurse - White Heat

CATHERINE SEYMOUR (Savage): Operative & Tango - Hide & Seek, Out Of Sight, and Hot Ice

CHAPMAN: Operative (PSI Unit) - Edge of Darkness

CONNOR JORDAN: Operative (PSI Unit) - Edge of Darkness

CONRAD CHRISTOF: Operative (In Australia) - Out Of Sight

CURTIS: (Deceased): Operative - The Mercenary

CURTNER: Operative & Trainer - Out of Sight

DAAN VILJOEN: Operative - Hot Ice

DARIUS (aka DARE): Operative - Hide & Seek, White Heat

DEKKER: Operative (PSI Unit) - Edge of Fear

DEREK WRIGHT: Operative - On Thin Ice, Out of Sight

DOYLE: Operative (Security Division) - White Heat

DUNCAN EDGE: Operative (PSI Unit) - Edge of Danger, Edge of Fear

FARRIS KEIR: Operative - Edge of Fear

FRANK FISK: Operative - Hot Ice

GABRIEL: Operative - Out Of Sight

GABRIEL EDGE: Operative (PSI Unit) - Edge of Darkness,Edge of Fear

GARDNER: Operative - Hot Ice

GARY LANDIS: Operative (PSI Unit) - Edge of Darkness

GREG SANDOVAL: Operative - White Heat

GUERRERO: Operative - White Heat

HOLLWELL: Operative - Hot Ice

DR. HOWARD: Doctor - White Heat

HUGO CALETTI: (Deceased) Operative - In Too Deep

HUNTINGTON ST. JOHN: Operative - Hot Ice, Kiss & Tell, On Thin Ice, In Too Deep, White Heat

IRIS: Nurse - White Heat

JAKE DOLAN: Operative - Kiss & Tell, Hide & Seek, On Thin Ice, Out of Sight, In Too Deep, Edge of Fear

JOE SKULLESTAD: (Deceased) Operative - Kiss & Tell

JUANITA SALAZAR: Operative (PSI Unit) - Edge of Darkness

KANE WRIGHT: Operative - Out of Sight, In Too Deep, Kiss & Tell, White Heat

KLEIVER: Operative - White Heat

KRISTA DAVIS: (Deceased) Operative - The Mercenary

KURTZ: (Deceased) Operative - White Heat

KYLE WRIGHT: Operative - Hide & Seek, In Too Deep, On Thin Ice, Out of Sight

LARK ORELA: Operative (PSI Unit) - Edge of Danger, Edge of Darkness, Edge of Fear

LEVINE: Operative - White Heat

MANNY ESCOBAR: Operative - Out Of Sight, Hot Ice

MARCUS SAVIN: Operative (Boss/CEO) - The Mercenary, White Heat

MAURO ZAMPIERI: (Deceased) Operative - White Heat

MAX ARIES: Operative - Hot Ice, White Heat

MCBRIDE: Operative - Out Of Sight

MICHAEL WRIGHT: Operative - In Too Deep, On Thin Ice, Kiss & Tell, Hide & Seek, Out of Sight

DR. MICHAEL YET: Doctor (HQ) - White Heat

MICHAELS: (Deceased) Operative - The Mercenary

MIKE RAGUSA: Operative (Security Division) - White Heat

NATASHA: Laundry (HQ) - White Heat

NAVARRO (Rafael): Operative - Hot Ice, White Heat, Ice Cold

NEAL BISHOP: Operative - Hot Ice

NIIGATA (Keiko): (Deceased) Operative - White Heat

NOAH HART: Operative (PSI Unit) - Edge of Darkness

PAUL BRITTON: (Deceased) Operative - Kiss & Tell

PAUL ROBERTS: Operative (Co-Pilot) - Hot Ice

PETER BLAINE: (Deceased) Operative (PSI Unit) - Edge of Darkness

PIET COATZEE: (Deceased) Operative - Hot Ice

RAYNARD ACKART: Operative - White Heat

REBECCA SANTOS: Tech girl - White Heat

RICHARD STRUBEN: (Deceased) Operative - Out of Sight

RIFKIN: Mailroom (Operative Trainee) - White Heat

ROMAN KILLIAN: Operative (In Cairo) - Out of Sight

ROSS LERMA: (Deceased) Operative (& Tango = Dancer) - Kiss & T ell

SAM PLUNKETT: (Deceased) Operative - Kiss & Tell

SAUL TANNENBAUM: Tech guy (Encryption Dept.) - White Heat

SAVAGE (CATHERINE SEYMOUR): Operative (& Tango) - Hide & Seek, Out Of Sight, Hot Ice

SEBASTIAN TREMAYNE: Operative - Edge of Danger, Edge of Darkness

SIMON PARRISH: Operative (PSI Unit) - Edge of Danger, Edge of Darkness

STAN BROWN: Operative (PSI Unit) - Edge of Darkness

TATE: Operative - Hot Ice

TAYLOR KINCAID: Operative - Hot Ice, White Heat

TES WONDWESEN: Operative (In Cairo) Out Of Sight

THOM LINDLEY: (Deceased) Operative (PSI Unit) - Edge of Danger, Edge of Darkness

TONY (Anthony) ROOK: Operative - Edge of Fear

UPTON FITZGERALD: Operative (PSI Unit) -Edge of Danger, Edge of Darkness

YANCY: Operative (PSI Unit) - Edge of Danger, Edge of Darkness

Cherry Adair Interview

Questions with New York Times & USA Today's Bestselling Author Cherry Adair

1. What is the best part of being a writer? What is the worst?

Best- The people I create can't tell me "No!" lol I love writing the second (3rd, 4th, 5th lol) draft. For me, writing the first draft is like building a house half a brick at a time with one arm tied behind my back and a blindfold on! Slow and painful. Unfortunately, at this stage of the process I have the attention span of a water newt, and can't seem to sit still for more than 15 agonizing minutes at a time. But once the walls are up, I'm filled with gusto, and then I'm obsessive about getting all the finish work done. Once a decorator, always a decorator.

I love the process of polishing and rewriting. I love the minutia of the last tweak, that last spit polish before sending it off to my editor. I even love revisions from my editor, because that gives me yet another shot at making the book shine.

Worst- That first draft. Erk! Not my fav. And having to be disciplined. It's hard on an Aries to plant her behind in that chair. I love to write, but sometimes the process of sitting down to write is painful.

2. Why do you write?

I can't. . .not. If I didn't get it all down on paper the voices in my head would mean I was crazy instead of creative.

3. Name one eye-opening thing you learned from your book research.

Snakes have two penises. (peni?) Not something that comes up in the normal course of conversation that often. (book: BLACK MAGIC)

4. Do you have a favorite motto?

Two. I love Mark Twain's: My books are like water; those of the great geniuses are wine. (Fortunately) everybody drinks water. And Gary Player's: -The harder you work, the luckier you get.

5. Do you have a favorite fictional hero? Favorite fictional heroine?

I'm pretty fickle. Whichever character I'm wring at the time is always my favorite. I must admit though that I do have a soft spot for Marc Savin (The Mercenary) because he was my first hero. We always remember our first. But currently I'm mad about Gideon Stark in GIDEON. He's the brother of Zak Stark (HUSH) I couldn't wait to see what really happened to him in the jungle when he and his brother separated after the kidnapping. And for much of the book, he doesn't know who he is or how he ended up where he ended up. SO much fun to write. I love writing jungle books (HIDE & SEEK, NIGHT FALL, TROPICAL HEAT, HUSH AND GIDEON. So far. Lol)I love exotic locals because to me the location is as much a character as my people.

As for a heroine, I adored Teal Williams. She was such a great foil for Zane, I've never written a heroine who is shy before. It was fascinating to get into her skin and see how she ticked.

6. Which fictional character would you hang out with?

Any of my heroes.

7. What is one of your favorite book covers, your own or someone else's?

I love the cover of WHIRLPOOL - Him- the splashing colors- him- the puzzled look- oh, yes, him.

8. What would readers be surprised to learn about you?

I'm pretty much an open book, so probably not much. I used to be an Interior Designer, I'm originally from Cape Town, South Africa. I love to read, enjoy playing in my garden (preferable after someone else has done the sweaty work) and can't not write every day. Spare time? What spare time?!

9. What's the strangest thing you've ever learned by Googling your name?

I'm a stripper. A fruit. A rude connotation A blossom. And a bomb. lol

10. If you could go backward or forward in time which would you chose? Why?

Back, because I'd know what was coming next.

11. Which do you find is most important to you as a writer, voice or story? Why? Hmm. Both. But if I had

to chose one - voice. Even if a story is well written, if the voice is dull and draggy, the book will be a snooze.

12. I know this is a difficult question with there being so many amazing authors out there to choose from but who are some of the GOT-TO-HAVE authors in your TBR pile?

I used to read a book a day. Now I'm lucky if I have time to finish a book in a month! That's the downside of doing what I do. I love being an author, but it's left me no time to enjoy one of my greatest pleasures. Some of my fav authors in no particular order - Ann Stuart, Maggie Osborne, Linda Howard. . .and dozens of others.

13. Are there discussion guides available for your books? Also, do you participate in author phone chats? And if so, how would my readers go about scheduling one?

Cherry: Yes, each book has a discussion guide available. Me, talk? Of course! (see above re: moderation)! I love talking with readers. The best way for you to get the discussion guides or arrange phone chats, or workshops is to contact me at Adairsupport@msn.com

14. You have so many awesome books out currently. How many have you published and when did you start your writing career?

A: I've published- hang on I have to count them. . . .63 I started writing long before I published. I wrote (and shredded) 17 books before The Mercenary came out in 1993

15. Since you live in the Northwest, where do you get your inspiration? Do you travel to the places in your books?

A: I have traveled to many of the exotic locals in my books, but not all of them. I don't like creepy-crawlies or not being anywhere near a shower or a flushing toilet! (and observant readers will notice that my heroines don't like the same things)

16. What other type of research do you do in order to start a book? Esp with the Black ops elements in your T-FLAC series?

A: I do extensive research - it's one of the most time consuming, and fun, aspects of writing for me. I'm lucky enough to have fans and friends in interesting places who fill me in on some of the local color first hand. When I'm doing research I try to find an expert in that field who is usually happy to answer all my question. Over the years I've made a lot of fascinating contacts because of my writing. (and a few very scary people, too!) I know several black ops guys who are incredibly monosyllabic in their answers, and it's like pulling hens teeth to get any kind of direct information out them. But once they got what I was writing, and that not only didn't I need to know troop movement in Iraq (or wherever, I really didn't want to know classified Intel) they were great at giving me other interesting factoids to make my operatives fun and interesting.

I met an interesting Ph.D nuclear physicist who helped me with info in CHAMELEON. A Venezuelan "business man" who loves my books, and has offered to help me with whatever I need (Let's leave it at that.

Lol) Jacques Cousteau's grandson, Fabien Cousteau (who is as yummy and delish as one of my heroes!) has helped with research for several of my books over the years. And I found a fascinating treasure hunter named Dr. Lubos Kordac who is helping me with details on salvaging for the Cutter Cay books. Over the course of 30 plus books I've collected a fascinating little black book filled with incredible and invaluable contacts. If I told you where I hide it I'd have to have one of my heroes (talk!!??) to you.

17. Is the T-FLAC series done now or will you continue those at some point?

A: I love my T-FLAC operatives, and yes, I will write them as long as readers love them as much as I do. My latest T-FLAC book is GIDEON, and I'm working very hard (OK obsessively!) on the two new trilogies which are not T-FLAC. (Although readers might see a familiar operative pop up where they least expect them.)

18. Do you have a favorite character you've written? Who gave you the most trouble?

A: I'm pretty fickle. Whichever character I'm wring at the time is always my favorite. I must admit though that I do have a soft spot **for Marc Savin (The Mercenary) because he was my first hero. We always remember our first.**

19. Who do you read? Favorite authors? Are you reading anything now?

A: I used to read a book a day. Now I'm lucky if I have time to finish a book in a month! That's the downside of doing what I do. I love being an author,

but it's left me no time to enjoy one of my greatest pleasures. Some of my fave authors in no particular order - Ann Stuart, Maggie Osbourn, Linda Howard. . . and dozens of others.

20. I know you like to take walks, what else do you do in your spare time?

A: I don't like to take walks! <g> I walk because it's good for me and gets me away from my computer for a bit of fresh air. Lol And what spare time?

21. Hollywood is calling!!! Who is playing the main characters in any one of your books?

A: The yummy and delicious Alex O'Loughlin (Hawaii Five-0) is my new TV crush. I'd pick him to play the role of Finn Gallagher. (Book: WHIRLPOOL) (I'd pick him to play…with me.)

Cherry, please tell us where we can find you in cyber world. For desperate readers like me, we just have to know…

I have lots of fun with readers on my Facebook, and Twitter pages, and I love hearing from readers through my web site www.cherryadair.com (where you can see pictures of ALL my heroes, read excerpts from my books, and find my complete booklist.)

About Cherry Adair

Always an adventurer in life as well as writing, New York Times best-selling author Cherry Adair moved halfway across the globe from Cape Town, South Africa to the United States in her early years to become an interior designer. She started what eventually became a thriving interior design business. "I loved being a designer because it was varied and creative, and I enjoyed working with the public." A voracious reader when she was able to carve out the time, Cherry found her brain crowded with characters and stories of her own.

"Eventually," she says, "the stories demanded to be told." Now a resident of the Pacific Northwest she shares the award- winning adventures of her fictional T-FLAC counter terrorism operatives with her readers. When asked why she chooses to write romantic action adventure, she says, "Who says you can't have adventure and a great love life? Of course, if you're talking about an adventurous love life, that's another thing altogether. I write romantic suspense coupled with heart-pounding adventure because I like to entertain, and nothing keeps readers happier than a rollercoaster read, followed by a happy ending."

Popular on the workshop circuit, Cherry gives lively classes on writing and the writing life. Pulling no punches when asked how to become a published writer, Cherry insists, "Sit your butt in the chair and write. There's no magic to it. Writing is hard work. It isn't for sissies or whiners."

Cherry loves to spend time at home. A corner desk keeps her focused-on writing, but the windows behind her, with a panoramic view of the front gardens, are always calling her to come outside and play. Her office has nine-foot ceilings, a fireplace, a television and built-in bookcases that house approximately 3,500 books.

"What can I say? My keeper shelf has been breeding in the middle of the night, rather like dry cleaners' wire clothes hangers."

More Novels by Cherry Adair

Look for these thrilling eBooks and print books on the Cherry Adair Online Bookstore or eBook retailers.

http://www.shop.cherryadair.com

CUTTER CAY SERIES

Undertow

Riptide

Vortex

Stormchaser

Hurricane

Whirlpool

FALLEN AGENTS OF T-FLAC Series

Absolute Doubt - Book 1

LODESTONE SERIES

Afterglow

Hush - Book 1

Gideon - Book 2

Relentless

T-FLAC SHORT STORIES

Playing for Keeps Enhanced

Ricochet

NOVELLA

A Killer Christmas - T-FLAC

PARANORMAL

Dark Prism

WRITER'S TOOLS

Cherry Adairs' Writers' Bible

Plotting by Color

Dialog

Character

Connect with Cherry on CherryAdair.com, Facebook, Pinterest, and Twitter, for info on new releases, access to exclusive offers, and much more!

Made in the USA
San Bernardino, CA
04 December 2018